THE P ARRANGEMENT

A RENDEZVOUS NOVEL

R.L. KENDERSON

THE P ARRANGEMENT

This book contains exhibitionism kink, degradation kink, accidental pregnancy, and a traumatic birth mentioned in the past.

To all our readers who started this journey with Vivian and Dominick, stayed for Rayne and Cade, and are still here for Delaney and Preston.
May you get all the D, the C, and P you want.

ONE

DELANEY

THROWING BACK MORE WINE THAN WHAT WAS considered ladylike, I tried to forget about what I had to do later tonight.

It didn't work.

But part of that could be because I was only allowing myself to have one glass before I broke the news to my friends that I wasn't staying for dinner.

I probably shouldn't have come to the restaurant at all because I wasn't in the best mood for socializing. But I'd promised my friend I would come to dinner so she could introduce me to her new boyfriend.

It didn't help that I had to watch my two friends, Rayne and Vivian, be blissfully happy with their partners while I sat alone at my end of the half-circular booth.

Rayne Thompson and Vivian Stern were my partners in the Women in Law project, started by the Minneapolis mayor, Nadine Evans. As a lawyer herself, she had started

Women in Law to educate girls and young women from elementary to high school about being a lawyer.

Rayne was a prosecutor for the county, Vivian was in the private sector, and I was a family court judge. Nadine was an associate of mine, and when she'd approached me, she had explained she was looking for a variety of careers people could pursue with a law degree to let the young women know there were many possibilities.

Since the project had started, Vivian, Rayne, and I had become closer, which was why Rayne wanted Vivian and me to meet Cade.

When I'd first met my new friends, Vivian had been single, and Rayne had been having troubles with her then boyfriend. Now, Vivian was living with Dominick, and a month after breaking up with her ex-boyfriend, Rayne was already in a serious relationship, judging by the "necklace" she wore around her neck.

Both women appeared to be in love with their partners. I was very happy for them, but it reminded me how alone I was. Not only was I the only single one, but I was also the oldest of the three, and after being married for over ten years and now divorced, I sometimes wondered if it was too late for me to find a happily ever after.

Most of the time, I was content with where I was in my life, but there were times when I was reminded of what I'd had.

And what I had lost.

"What do you do for work, Cade?" I asked to get my mind off of feeling sorry for myself.

Cade sat with his arm around Rayne and smiled down at her, and she beamed back up at him. The relationship had seemed to come out of nowhere, but it was obvious how the two of them felt about one another.

"I am a manager at the Iron House," Cade said. "But Rayne's brother, Beau, and I are going to be opening up our own restaurant hopefully within the next year. I'll run the place, and Beau will be our head chef."

"It'll be a lot of work, but I think Cade and my brother are going to love having their own place."

"Congratulations," Vivian said as she leaned into Dominick.

"That sounds very exciting," I said. "You'll have to invite us to your grand opening."

"Of course you'll be invited," Rayne said, pushing her hair off her shoulder.

Vivian touched her neck as she looked at our friend. "Rayne, is that new?"

Rayne stiffened, and her eyes widened as Cade smirked. "Yes." It practically came out as a squeak, and I had to purse my lips so I didn't laugh.

When it came to my two friends, they were opposites. Vivian was reserved when it came to her feelings, to the point some people thought she was cold. Whereas Rayne was a person who was almost always in a good mood, and every emotion she felt showed on her face.

"It's beautiful," Vivian told Rayne.

Vivian had loosened up since dating Dominick, but she

was still blunt sometimes. In this case, she was bluntly clueless.

Dominick put his mouth to her ear, and I was close enough to hear him say, "Baby, that isn't a necklace."

Vivian frowned and, in a voice much louder than her boyfriend's, asked, "Then, what is it?"

Dominick shook his head with a laugh. He was also the opposite of Vivian. Almost scruffy and tattooed. He looked like a bad boy next door to Vivian's clean-cut, professional style.

"It's a submissive collar," he said in a hushed voice.

Vivian's face flushed red. "I—I—oh my God. I didn't—"

I couldn't hold back my laughter anymore. For as long as I'd known her, I had never seen Vivian so flustered before.

She whipped her head toward me. "So, you knew what it was?"

I grinned. "Of course I did."

Looking at Rayne, I raised my glass. "Congratulations." I could totally see my friend as a submissive and being very content in the role.

Rayne's scarlet color rivaled Vivian's. "Thank you. But it's not what you think. He's not my dom, and I'm not his sub. He just likes to be in control in the bedroom." She looked down, a slow smile forming on her face. "And I like it when he is."

Cade growled, "Also, it's because you're mine, Rayne."

She immediately met his eyes. "Yeah, I am." Her voice was almost breathless.

"Maybe I should put one of those on you, baby," Dominick said to Vivian.

She stared at her boyfriend and swallowed. A few beats later, she muttered, "I don't think so."

Dominick chuckled. "I like that you actually thought about it for a moment."

Scowling, Vivian narrowed her eyes. "No, I didn't."

She totally had, but Dominick just smiled and kissed her nose. He knew when not to argue with his hardheaded girlfriend.

Vivian turned to me. "What about you, Delaney? Is that something you would ever wear? Or did you ever wear one for your ex?"

I snorted at the thought. "No."

I was neither a submissive nor a dominant. I was somewhere in the middle. I had loved it when my ex told me I was his, like Cade had just done with Rayne. But he could only boss me around for a limited time before my strong-willed personality had enough.

However, that hadn't stopped me from letting my ex put his claim on me in another way.

But it was private, not in a place everyone could see, like Rayne.

And with that thought, it seemed like it was time for me to go.

I sipped my last bit of wine and set my glass on the table. "It was very nice meeting you, Cade, but I need to head out."

Rayne's face fell. "What? You just got here."

"I know, and I'm sorry."

"Was it something I said?" Vivian asked. "I shouldn't have said anything about your ex."

Shaking my head with a grin, I gathered my phone and purse. "No," I said with a sigh. "Paxton's nanny had to leave town. I'm not sure how long she'll be gone. Her mother had to have spinal surgery, and Madison went to take care of her for a while."

"Oh my God." Sympathy was written all over Rayne's face.

"It's okay. Her mom is doing well. I'm just out of a nanny for a few weeks at least."

"What are you doing with Paxton?" Vivian asked.

"My sister, Natalie, is watching him for the time being."

My younger sister was a PRN nurse, which meant she only worked when the hospital needed her. She was only responsible for picking up two shifts a month, leaving her to be a stay-at-home mom the rest of the time. While I really appreciated her help, I also felt guilty for giving her extra work when she already had two kids of her own. One of which was a baby.

"Which means I need to pick him up." I had come to dinner right after leaving the courthouse, which meant my son had been there all day.

Rayne frowned. "But I thought this was your ex's weekend. That's why I scheduled it for today." Her shoulders slumped. "Did I get it mixed up?"

Scooting to the edge of the booth, I shook my head and

gave her a reassuring smile. "No. You got it right. But usually, Madison takes Paxton back and forth to my house and Preston's, so without her, I have to drop him off."

"Can't Preston pick him up from your sister's?" Vivian asked.

"He could, but it's best if he doesn't. My sister isn't his biggest fan."

Despite being my little sister, she was very protective of me. Natalie was one of the reasons I'd made it through my divorce as well as I did.

"Neither are you," Vivian pointed out.

I snort-laughed. "Yeah, but my sister didn't marry Preston and have his baby. I did, which means this is my responsibility. Also, I need to talk to my ex about switching weekends so I can go to that law conference in Vegas. Madison *was* going to watch him that weekend to make some extra money, but obviously, that plan's not going to work out. And I can't cancel because I'm supposed to be doing a presentation."

Rayne smiled sympathetically at me. "I didn't even think about your conference. Good luck, Delaney."

I stood and flung my purse over my shoulder. "Thanks. I'm going to need it."

TWO
DELANEY

THE GOOD PART ABOUT MY SISTER BABYSITTING MY two-and-a-half-year-old was that he hadn't wanted to leave when I came to pick him up. I was happy he had so much fun playing with his cousins. It made me feel less guilty about leaving him there all day.

Natalie had a son a year older than mine and a daughter a year younger, and Paxton always loved playing with his older cousin. It was times like these when I felt regret that I would probably never give my son a sibling. I was getting up in age, and after adding in dating, an engagement, and marriage, it would be a long time before I could possibly be pregnant. *If* I even met someone. And I knew I didn't have to be married to have another child, but being a single parent to one was hard enough. I didn't think I could handle a second.

On the flip side, the bad part about my sister babysitting my son was that he hadn't wanted to leave when I came to pick him up.

So far, my ex and I had been cordial with each other, but I didn't want to find out what happened if I was late for his drop-off time.

Finally, I had told Paxton he was going to see his dad, and just like that, he had run to me to help him put on his shoes.

And now, I was the one who needed some coaxing.

"Mommy, go inside. See Daddy."

Lifting my eyes to the rearview mirror, I looked at Paxton. "Okay, bud. Can you just give Mommy a couple more seconds?"

Since the divorce, I had managed to see my ex-husband only a handful of times, and every time I did, I still felt the ache in my chest. It wasn't nearly as strong as it had been the day I left him, but it was still there.

One would think that after a year, I would be over losing the man I loved, but it still hurt. I was living for the day when I was well and truly over him.

Unfortunately, that day was not today.

And seeing the home I had lived in for ten years—nine and a half of them wonderful—only made it worse.

"No, Mommy. Now."

"Paxton," I warned.

He was starting to get more demanding, and I was doing my best to turn him into a polite young man.

"*Pease.*"

I couldn't stop the smile from spreading across my face.

I loved how he said please, and I was going to be sad when he was able to pronounce all the letters correctly.

"Okay, baby. Let's get you inside."

I exited my vehicle, unhooked Paxton from his car seat, and let him go to run to the front door while I trailed behind.

"Ring the doorbell," I called to him.

But rather than listening to me, Paxton grabbed for the door handle. I wasn't worried until he actually managed to open the door. It just had to be one of those levers that made it easy for a toddler to pull down.

Picking up my pace, I hurried toward my son. I had no idea where my ex was in the house, and I worried Paxton could get hurt if he didn't have an adult to watch him. Lately, he'd become too curious about things without any consideration for his well-being. Such was life with a toddler.

Thankfully, he was on the floor, pulling off his shoes when I reached him.

He threw the second one down, climbed to his feet, and yelled, "Daddy."

My body tensed, going on alert as I waited to see where my ex would pop out from while I tried to shut out the memories flooding me.

I knew this house so well, and the fact that it looked like nothing had changed since I'd left was a surprise as well as a punch to the gut. It hurt to look at everything I'd left behind because, for some reason, in my head, I had pictured Preston doing a complete redecoration to erase all traces of me.

Preston had inherited the house from his parents when they retired, and when I moved in, we did a major overhaul of the old-fashioned furniture and outdated wallpaper. I had just assumed he would do the same thing when I left.

Snapping myself out of my depressing thoughts, I looked around for my ex.

To the right was his study and the stairs leading to the second floor, and to the left was the living room. But I should have been focusing straight ahead to the dining room, where it led to the kitchen because there he was in all his masculine glory.

Preston St. James III.

My ex-husband, the father of my child, and still the one and only love of my life.

Unfortunately, after the birth of our child, I'd stopped being his.

The word *craggy* always came to mind when I thought of Preston, but it was his mouth that had always done me in. It was a little too wide and his lips a little too thick, but I had always loved them and thought they were the absolute sexiest things about my ex-husband. And that was saying something because Preston was tall and muscular with broad shoulders. And despite having a thick head of dirty-blond hair, his face was almost always dusted with a permanent dark five-o'clock shadow that matched his brown eyes. He had on black slacks that had been tailor-made for his ass, a black tie that was undone and hanging off his shoulders, and a white dress shirt he had unbuttoned halfway down his chest. I hated that I could see his smooth, muscular chest and the North Star necklace he wore between his pecs, but I hated even more that my breath still caught when I saw him.

"Hey, buddy." He beamed at our son, who ran toward him, arms out wide, while not giving me a second glance.

The twinge was back, and I rubbed my sternum as Preston swung Paxton up in his arms. Kissing him on the forehead, he finally looked at me.

"Delaney," he said with not even a hint of warmth.

I straightened my back. "Preston."

Remembering I'd come here to convince him to switch weekends with me, I forced a smile onto my face. "I was hoping to talk to you about something."

His eyebrows flew up as Paxton started to wiggle in his arms.

"I hungry, Daddy."

Preston set him down. "Okay, buddy."

Paxton ran over to me, grabbed my hand, and tugged. "Come, Mommy. I eat."

Looking down at my son, I couldn't help but smile. Even though he looked just like his father, enough to make my heart ache, I still loved the kid to death.

I held up a finger and didn't budge from my spot. "One second. Mommy needs to talk to Daddy."

Squaring my shoulders, I looked up at my ex.

"Can I talk to you for a minute?"

THREE
PRESTON

I had half a mind to tell Delaney to leave and that I didn't want to talk to her when texting had been working for us so far.

I hated having to see her.

Every time was like a punch to the gut. Even after two years.

We'd been apart for about two years, yet I still wanted her as much as the day we'd said *I do*, and I resented the fact that I could no longer touch her like I used to. Like I still wanted to.

Her shoulders squared when I didn't answer right away, and I relented. As much as I hated seeing her, the reality was, I didn't hate *her* at all.

Not even a little bit.

And it hurt me to see how strong she was trying to be in front of me.

Her thick brown hair fell past her shoulders over her

blue blouse. Delaney had always been what she described as "midsize" with thicker hips that I used to love to grab and a soft belly that I used to love to touch. She wore a pencil skirt that came to her knees, which accentuated her curves just right, along with a pair of heels. She looked like the professional judge she was, except for her eyes. She looked weary, and the normal green sparkle I was used to was missing. Despite that, she was still the most beautiful woman in the world.

And even in my frustration, I didn't have it in me to tell her no to her question.

"Sure. But come into the kitchen so I can feed Pax."

I spun on my heel and didn't wait to see if she followed. Pulling a small bowl from the cupboard, I saw Paxton bolt past me to the kitchen table. He was big enough now to climb up onto his booster seat. We left it strapped to a kitchen chair, where we always ate since I never used the dining room. It reminded me of growing up and all my parents' stuffy guests and fancy dinners, where I'd had to be quiet and sit still, as if I were a mini adult instead of a kid.

"What did you want to talk about?" I asked my ex-wife as I walked over to the stove.

Glancing at her over my shoulder, I caught her staring at the skillet sitting on the burner. My housekeeper, Clara, had made dinner for Paxton and me before leaving for the evening.

"Is that Clara's pasta?"

I turned away, hiding my forming smile. "The one and only."

She groaned, and the sound of pleasure from deep in her throat had my dick growing hard behind my zipper.

That was enough to wipe the grin off my face.

"I love Clara's pasta." Her voice was filled with longing in a way only good food could do.

"I know." I dished up a small portion for Paxton.

"Mommy, stay. Mommy eat wiff me and Daddy."

"Oh, honey, Mommy can't—"

I turned around. "If you want to eat, you can stay."

I didn't really want her to, but I couldn't say no to my son. He rarely saw both of his parents at the same time, and it just didn't seem fair to him that we had gotten divorced.

Delaney's eyes widened in surprise, but I knew her well enough to know she wanted to say yes.

"You know where the dishes are. You're more than welcome to help yourself."

I tried to ignore her moving around my kitchen like she used to and focused on getting Paxton his dinner. After putting his bowl down in front of him, I grabbed him a glass of milk and dished up my own food.

"How was visiting your cousins today, Pax?" I asked as I put his milk on the table.

"Fun." His eyes sparkled, and I grinned.

"Thank you for asking your sister to help out," I said to Delaney as she sat down across from me.

I often envied her relationship with her sister and

parents. My own had never been very warm toward me, and as an only child, I had no one else. For a while, I had been close to my in-laws.

I missed them almost as much as I missed my ex-wife.

"I'm just grateful we have her," she said.

I swallowed at her use of the word *we*.

"I'm sure we could have found a day care or some- thing," she added. "Or maybe even a temporary nanny if we needed to."

"I'm still appreciative because we know we can't ask my mother, and I don't really have anyone else."

Delaney's lips curled even though she tried to hide it.

She had never liked my mother, and to be honest, I couldn't blame her. Both my parents had come from more money than Delaney's family, and my mother always looked down on her. My father hadn't been as bad, but he had passed away six years ago.

After our divorce, my mother had moved in with me to help out with Paxton, and that had been a disaster. She was impolite to Paxton's nanny, and she really did nothing to help. Plus, she always had rude comments to make about Delaney whenever she dropped him off or picked him up. At times, I felt like I had two children.

When she'd decided to go on a spontaneous trip out of the country with her friends, I'd told her it was best that she move out. Paxton needed more stability than her coming and going as she pleased, especially if it came to last-minute changes in his schedule because she had decided to go on vacation. Thankfully, she agreed, and

Paxton's nanny was bumped up to full-time. Things had been a lot more peaceful ever since. I suspected she hadn't wanted to move in with me in the first place.

I hadn't told Delaney that my mother was coming to town tomorrow and was going to babysit while I went on a date she'd set up for me. I had half a mind to cancel because I didn't really want to go out with anyone, especially someone my mother wanted me to get involved with. But it was better than staying home with my mother all night, and it kept her off my back. If I gave her the illusion I was trying to find a new wife, she would leave me alone. And since I would put Paxton to bed before I left, I trusted her enough to watch him while he was sleeping. But her watching him all day while he bounced off the walls would never happen.

"As a nurse, Natalie understands how much care Madison's mother needs, so she is happy to do it." She looked at our son and smiled. "I think she might actually like it a little. Paxton and Cooper played all afternoon. It actually gave her a little bit of a break."

Her face suddenly fell, and she looked down at her food.

I frowned at the abrupt change of expression, but when Delaney took her first bite of pasta and moaned, my mood unexpectedly changed from concerned to turned on.

"Oh my God. I knew Clara's pasta tasted good, but it's even better than I remembered." She shut her eyes and licked her lips.

My dick ached.

R.L. KENDERSON

Once upon a time, I would have pushed all the dishes to one side, pulled her on top of the table, and fucked her right there.

I gritted my teeth and tried not to think about sex, but it was hard when my ex looked like she was seconds away from an orgasm.

"*Delaney*," I snapped.

She opened her eyes, a questioning look on her face.

"Paxton said something to you," I lied.

"What did you need, baby?" she asked him.

Paxton, oblivious to my torture, shrugged and said, "Nofin'."

Thankfully, Delaney just laughed, probably thinking our almost three-year-old had forgotten what he was going to say.

I shoveled the rest of my food in my mouth and stood. "I'm going to clean up the kitchen."

Delaney's eyes widened. "You're finished already?"

"Yep." Picking up my fork and plate, I shoved my chair to the table.

"Is everything okay?"

I gave her a fake smile. "Yeah. I just like to get it done sooner rather than later," I said and headed for the dishwasher.

Hopefully, when I was done putting all the food and dishes away, she'd be finished eating and stop torturing me with her presence.

FOUR
DELANEY

Frowning, I sighed down at my food and shook my head.

"Mommy okay?"

"Yeah, buddy," I lied.

Preston getting up from the table so soon had brought back memories of the time before I left him. I was trying hard to move on, but it was difficult when he reminded me of my hurt and anger.

But dwelling on that would get me nowhere, so I forced a smile for my son. "I get to eat Clara's yummy food. How could I not be okay?"

And the food truly was delicious. Obviously, losing my husband and best friend had been a huge blow, but I sure missed Clara and her excellent cooking too.

"Yummy, yummy," Paxton said with a giggle.

I grabbed a napkin from the holder on the table and

couldn't help but chuckle, too, because the kid had sauce all over his face.

"All done," he said, showing me his bowl.

It was empty.

"Good job. Do you want any more?"

"No. Want milk."

I handed his glass to him and finished off my own pasta. Out of the corner of my eye, I saw him trying to put his milk back on the table, and almost as if in slow motion, it fell over and spilled everywhere.

"*Oh shit*," I yelped, jumping up from the table to grab Paxton.

But it was too late. He was already covered in milk.

I hadn't even realized Preston had seen what happened until he brought over a towel to soak up the spill, and I was almost startled by the smile on his face.

"Oh, buddy, you made a mess."

Paxton laughed. "I messy."

"Yeah, you are," I told him. If we were at home, I knew exactly what I would do. "Do you care if I take him upstairs and give him a bath?" I asked my ex.

"Or should we just throw the kid out and start all over?" Preston paused in his wiping off the table and grinned up at me.

I was stunned at him joking with me, so it took me a couple of seconds to tease back. "Tempting, but we've already put almost three years of work into this one."

Maybe I had jumped to conclusions before, when he

got up from the table so soon. Maybe he really had wanted to clean up.

Preston picked up the drenched towel and held it over his cupped hand in case it dripped. As he made his way over to the sink, he said, "Go give him a bath while I clean up here." As I headed out, he added, "I usually put him in the tub in our room. He likes it because it's bigger."

I froze, waiting for Preston to realize he had called his bedroom *our room*, but when I looked back at him, he was busy wringing the milk out of the towel in the sink.

Sitting on the floor in my old bathroom and watching my son play in the bathtub felt surreal. Truthfully, this whole night had been surreal. I had lived in this house, used this bathroom, slept in the bed out there for more years than my current home. It was supposed to be where my ex and I were going to raise our children. It was no wonder it felt surreal.

"I got the kitchen cleaned up, including Paxton's seat," Preston said, walking into the bathroom. He held up two articles of clothing. "Here are Pax's PJs." He set them on the counter and leaned against it.

"Oh, good. It's probably time for him to get out."

Our son yawned.

"Definitely time for him to get out," I corrected.

I stood, and without thinking, I opened up the linen closet and pulled out a towel like I'd done a million times before. As I closed the door, I wondered if I should have asked first, but at the same time, it seemed silly to ask when Paxton needed a towel and I knew where they were.

I mentally shrugged. It was too late now.

"Okay, buddy, it's time to get out."

Paxton looked up at me with all the confidence of a toddler. "No."

"Yes," I said, using a sterner voice.

He looked at his father and back at me. "No."

I counted to ten because I knew he was tired. Arguing with him never got me anywhere when he was sleepy, but it was hard to not show my frustration. I was exhausted too.

Preston pushed himself off the counter. "Paxton, it's time to get out."

He looked his father right in the eye. "No."

Preston and I exchanged glances, and I could tell he was thinking the same thing I was. *What the hell are we going to do with him?*

I had to purse my lips so I didn't laugh.

Being a single parent could be hard, and it was nice to know I wasn't alone, especially when it came to the same kid.

Facing our wayward child, I shrugged and said in my best nonchalant voice, "Okay, you have fun here." I hung up the towel on the rack. "I'm going to go read Daddy a bedtime story since you would rather stay in the tub."

Preston made a sound beside me, but when I turned to him, he was already acting for Paxton's benefit. "Ooh, I love bedtime stories." He rubbed his hands together. "Let me go grab a book."

"*No.*" Paxton scrambled up. "I get story."

I pretended to not understand. "Does this mean you want to get out?"

"*Yes.*" His little brow furrowed.

"Oh, okay."

I pulled the towel from the rack, and when Paxton spun around for me to wrap it around his back, Preston gave me a fist bump.

I had to hide my smile from Paxton when he turned back around. Thankfully, he was too focused on getting out of the bathtub and putting his pajamas on to realize he wasn't the one who'd won.

His father and I walked him to his room.

"Okay, buddy, give Mommy a hug and kiss so you can lie down."

I still hadn't talked to Preston about switching weekends, but Paxton needed to go to bed. And I was beginning to think it would be easier to take my sister up on her offer to watch him. Preston and I had gotten along tonight. I didn't want to ruin that by asking for a favor.

Paxton frowned. "Read story, Mommy." Unlike in the tub, his voice was sad and confused.

"Daddy's going to read you a story." I got down on my haunches and took his hands. "Mommy's going to read you a story when I see you on Sunday."

He let go of my hands and wrapped his little arms

around my neck. "No, Mommy. Read story to me and Daddy."

Oh man. How was I supposed to resist him when he was being so adorable?

Wrapping my arms around him, I hugged him tight. "Mommy—"

"Will read a story to both of us. And then Daddy will read a story to you and Mommy," Preston said.

I looked up at him and mouthed, *Are you sure?*

He smiled and nodded.

"Did you hear that?" I said to Paxton. "You get two stories."

"Yay!" He let me go and ran over to his full-size bed. It looked enormous around him, but he'd grow into it someday.

He patted the mattress on one side of him. "Mommy lay here." And then he patted the other side. "Daddy lay here."

Relief hit me because I hadn't even thought about him possibly suggesting that his father and I lie down next to each other. I wouldn't have wanted another argument with Paxton, but I also didn't know if I could have lain on a bed beside my ex without needing a long therapy session after.

Preston and I got on the bed with our son, and he handed me a book.

"We've been reading this one a lot lately."

I nodded and read the title. "Does this work, Pax?"

He nodded, and I began to read.

I hoped that before I was finished, Paxton would fall

asleep. Although he was clearly tired, when I closed the book, he was still awake.

"Daddy's turn."

So, while Preston found something else to read, I settled in next to Paxton. I always missed him when he was with his dad, so I made sure to enjoy these last few minutes together.

Preston started the second book, and I could feel myself nodding off toward the end, but before I knew it, he said the words, *"The End."*

I lifted my gaze to see him smiling down at our son, the love showing clearly from his eyes.

It made my heart clench.

"He's out."

"Oh, good." My voice came out tighter than I'd wanted it to. I cleared my throat and carefully stood. "That's our cue to leave."

It was also my cue to leave the house.

I kissed Paxton on the forehead and brushed my hand over his head. "I'll see you in a couple of days, sweetheart," I whispered.

Reluctantly, I pulled away and rounded his bed toward the half-closed bedroom door as Preston turned off the lamp next to the bed. While the sun was going down and there was a bit of light peeking from underneath the blinds and curtain, it was not enough to show the toy in my path. Of course, I tripped.

More afraid of waking Paxton than getting hurt if I crashed into something, I reached for the nearest thing.

My ex-husband.

Preston caught me before I crashed into the bed, and we both froze. With a quick look to see if our son was still sleeping, he kicked the truck out of the way, and we hurried out the door, silently laughing the whole way.

"Holy crap, that was close," I told him when we slipped out of the room.

Preston reached behind me to close the door and grinned. "I thought for sure you were going down."

I put my palms on his chest. "Thanks for saving me." My heart was racing from my near fall.

A click sounded behind me, and Preston shifted his eyes to my hands as his smile slowly slipped from his face.

When he lifted his chin, I wasn't prepared to see the heat in them, and my heart started pounding for a whole other reason.

As if we shared a thought, our mouths crashed together as we wrapped our arms around each other. I parted my lips, and Preston plunged his tongue inside. I groaned at the taste of him. It was familiar and welcoming in a way I hadn't felt in way too long.

And that was what lifted the sexual cloud that had descended on my brain.

I needed to stop this before I got hurt again, and without a second thought, I slipped from his arms and bolted down the stairs.

FIVE
DELANEY

I RUSHED TO THE KITCHEN AFTER FLEEING FROM Preston upstairs. It infuriated me that I was being such a chicken, but a series of rejections could do that to even the most confident woman.

My purse was lying where I'd left it on the counter when he invited me to stay and eat, but instead of grabbing it and running out the front door, I found myself at the back of the room in front of the sliding glass door.

Wrapping my arms around myself, I stared out into the backyard as I tried to catch my breath. It was twilight, and I noted Paxton's swing set and his sandbox and the lights flickering on in the neighbors' houses. But it did nothing to block out the footsteps coming up behind me.

Really, I felt him more than heard Preston, and when he stopped at my back, I held my breath.

I had no idea what he was going to do, and I had the fleeting thought that I should have left.

I knew he would never hurt me. Physically at least. My heart was a whole different story.

My hair was swept off my shoulder, Preston's strong hand grazing my neck, and I shuddered. Not just from the chill of the air hitting me, but also at what was going to come next. I couldn't stop myself from closing my eyes and arching my neck even if it meant he might turn me away again.

Preston stepped closer, our bodies now touching. The light caress of his fingertips started at the sensitive area under my ear and slid down over my shoulder.

I swallowed hard.

He continued over my sternum and the top of my breast. Just as he wrapped his other arm around my middle, he tore the top of my blouse apart, the upper buttons scattering everywhere.

With a growl, he slipped his hand under my bra and latched on to my nipple just as he bit down on my neck.

I cried out and grabbed on to the back of his head, holding him to me. I had wanted this for so long. I was terrified he'd stop.

Preston sucked on my shoulder and kneaded my breast, pinching my nipple every few seconds.

My core clenched, and my panties grew wet. I pushed my ass against his cock and rubbed when I found it hard.

Preston groaned as the arm around my middle went to the bottom of my skirt, and he yanked on it, trying to lift it up.

Not wanting the thick material in the way of him

touching me, I made quick work of the clasp and zipper on my side.

As soon as it was on the floor, Preston's hand was ripping away my underwear. And when his hand landed between my legs, he froze at what he found there.

"It doesn't mean anything," I told him.

"The fuck it doesn't." He thumbed my clit piercing. "Although I suppose you took it out and replaced it by now."

I bit down on my bottom lip.

"Doesn't matter. I'm still the one who put it there in the first place."

The day we'd gotten engaged, Preston had taken us to a tattoo shop, wanting us to put our names on each other. I told him absolutely not because it was bad luck. Couples always broke up or got divorced.

But since I'd always wanted the hood of my clitoris pierced, I let him do that. And when I say I let him do that, I mean, the piercer prepped me and lined the needle up, but when it came time to push it through, he let Preston do it with his hand over Preston's.

Actually, the piercer had asked Preston if he wanted to be the one to do it after my then fiancé stood in the corner, staring at another man touching me in a place he thought of as only his to touch. I couldn't lie that it was hot as fuck, and we went home and screwed like rabbits later that night. We stayed away from the positions that might hurt, but it didn't stop us from doing it all night.

After I had gotten my new piercing, I had tried to

convince Preston to do the same thing to his penis—not only to avoid jinxing our relationship, but also because it would be awesome to feel—but he'd been set on a tattoo. So, he put my name on his left ribs, and I had to admit, it was sexy as hell. I used to run my fingers over it when we were in bed together. Unfortunately, in the end, I had been right because, now, we were no longer together, and I was sure he'd had that tattoo removed months ago.

I'd had grand plans to remove my piercing several times because it made me think of Preston, but every time I'd tried, I hadn't been able to go through with it. Hell, I couldn't even make myself change

"No point in you not enjoying it," he said, knocking my thoughts out of the past and back to the present.

He was right. I couldn't change what had happened between us, but I could enjoy Preston here and now.

"Exactly." It was as good of a reason as any for me to keep my piercing.

"Then, let's show the neighbors your pretty pussy while I make you come."

I moaned and bucked my hips against his hand.

I felt him smile against my ear.

"Still the same. You're such a slut, Delaney, wanting everyone to see you soak my hand as you orgasm all over it." He nipped my ear. "Aren't you?"

"Yes," I admitted with a hiss.

God, I loved it when he called me a slut. Not very feminist of me, but just hearing the word come out of his mouth had me dripping.

Preston and I might be divorced, but the man knew me better than anyone. And he knew how much I loved the idea of someone watching me. Of someone catching us in the act.

But he also understood how bad it would be for either of us to actually be found with our pants literally down, due to our careers. He always knew how to turn me on without either of us losing our jobs.

It was one of the reasons I loved him.

Used to love him, I corrected.

Either way, not many men were comfortable with giving in to my desires, like Preston had been. Trust me, I had tried to find them. Before and after him.

"Spread your legs and arch your ass, Laney." Preston pushed two fingers into me and pressed his thumb against my clit, under my piercing. Knowing my body so well, he hit my G-spot without even trying and used the exact amount of pressure on my swollen nub. "Fuck, Delaney, you're already going to come."

He was right.

He tugged on my nipple and twisted. "So tight and wet."

I whimpered, tingles starting to form between my legs.

"Still the best cunt." He sucked on my neck and whispered, "Still my favorite cunt."

It couldn't be true, but my sex-hazed brain didn't care because the tingles turned into full-on tremors as my climax seized control of my body, crashing through me.

Preston held me close as my legs gave out underneath me, and I gasped for air.

I hadn't orgasmed like that since before Paxton was born. Not even by my own hand.

God, did it feel good.

Preston stole his hand from between my thighs and swiped his fingers over my bottom lip. "Open, Delaney," he commanded.

But I already knew what he wanted, and I sucked him into my mouth before he even finished. I got off on the idea of people watching us. He got off on me tasting myself after he made me come.

"My turn," he growled.

"Your turn?"

With several smooth movements, Preston was facing me and moving me away from the sliding door, toward the very table we'd just eaten dinner off of. With a small nudge, he pushed me to lie back.

Stretching my legs wide, I was grateful the sun had just gone down and the closest light was out in the front hall so he couldn't see between my pussy well. I didn't want him to know how much he still meant to me. Not with me almost completely naked while he was dressed. And not after he had just played my body like an instrument he'd been practicing his whole life.

"My turn to watch." He ran a fingertip up my slit. "And my turn to taste." He leaned over my body, taking my breasts in his big, strong hands as his mouth hovered over my cleft. "I've fucking missed your taste," he muttered right before his thick, beautiful lips descended on my pussy like he was trying to devour me.

He licked and sucked on every inch of my flesh, to the point I was squirming on the hard wood under me. One would think after having such a great orgasm, I wouldn't be aching again so soon, but the man knew what he was doing.

"Please, Pres."

He looked up at me. "Please what, Laney?"

My chest heaving, I debated on saying anything. After all, in the past, it had gotten me nowhere.

Preston circled my clit with his tongue. "Please what?" he whispered, and I gave in.

"Please make me come. Please fuck me. Please just do something to end this torture."

With a chuckle, he flicked my nub and wrapped his mouth around it. Then, he did the thing that we both loved. With his top lip over my piercing, he put my clit in between it and his tongue and sucked as he hummed.

My back arched off the table as I flew over the edge a second time that night.

"Fuck, fuck, fuck," I yelled, not caring if my voice was loud enough to wake a sleeping child.

I was still coming off my climactic high when he lifted his head and used one hand to rip open his pants. He wrapped his fists around the top of my thighs as he yanked me to the edge and practically impaled me on his thick cock.

"*Fuck.*" Preston held me to him as he paused and looked up at the ceiling.

He'd gotten rid of his tie long ago, but his dress shirt was still open, and I stared in amazement and lust as his tanned chest heaved beneath it.

I pushed myself up and kissed his bare skin on one pectoral and then the next.

His dick jerked inside me, and I smiled.

Tracing my lips across his clavicle, I made my way up to his ear and whispered, "Fuck me, Preston. Fuck me so hard—"

Preston shoved me down, dropping over me as he withdrew, and slammed back into me.

"*Yes,*" I cried out, clutching at his back.

Cupping my head in his hands, he held us nose to nose as he relentlessly drove into me, thrust after thrust, in the perfect position for my piercing to rub my clit to make me come.

"I want to come in you, Laney."

I nodded.

"Do I have anything to worry about?"

Confused, I shook my head. If he was concerned about STIs, it was too late since he wasn't using any protection. And he couldn't be concerned about pregnancy. He had already taken care of that.

"No," I answered anyway.

I had only been with two men since our divorce, one time each—neither had me wanting a repeat performance

—and I'd used condoms with both of them and gotten tested afterward.

"Good," he growled and kissed me.

His tongue swept into my mouth, and I tasted myself on him.

He lifted his mouth, his gaze full of determination. "Because I want to coat your cunt with my cum until I'm leaking out of you."

I whimpered and tightened around him involuntarily.

"You want that too, huh?" It wasn't really a question. "Slutty Delaney wants me to come inside her. She wants me to mark her with my seed." He dropped his forehead to mine, looked me in the eye, and said the words he knew would get me off. "That's because she's my slut."

Crying out, I dug my nails into Preston's back so hard that it probably ruined my overly expensive manicure, but I couldn't care less. The orgasm that ripped through every nerve in my body was worth it as wave after wave of pleasure crashed over me.

Preston kissed me again, still holding my head, as he shoved into me one last time, hurtling himself over the edge with me and flooding my pussy with his cum.

After a minute or two, we both lay there, him draped over me, as we tried to catch our breaths.

Preston lifted himself up onto his hands and stared at me a moment. But rather than say anything, he hauled me into his arms, his cock still inside me.

"What are you doing?"

Not only did I not know where he was taking me, but I also wasn't a small woman. I kept myself trim, but I was still midsize and not exactly light.

Yet Preston didn't seem fazed. "I'm taking you upstairs. You and I aren't done for the night."

SIX

DELANEY

I woke up to the familiar feeling of a little arm and leg thrown over me and smiled. No matter how many times I put Paxton to bed in his own room on the nights he stayed with me, at least half the time, I woke up with him in my own bed.

When he'd first transitioned to his big-boy bed, I used to wake up when he crawled in with me. He wasn't either stealthy or quiet, and I would send him back to his own room. But the kid was smart, and he had realized if I stayed asleep, I wouldn't kick him out. And I liked when he snuggled up next to me, so I couldn't really be mad at him for coming into my room. He was only going to be little for a short time. He wouldn't want to cuddle with his mommy forever.

Pushing the covers off my face, careful not to disturb Paxton, I blinked at my surroundings and froze. I recognized everything in the room, but the thing was, it was no longer *my* room, and panic slowly began to sink in at what I had done last night.

I'd had sex—a whole ton of sex—with my ex-husband.

I winced. *What the hell was I thinking?*

I didn't really need to answer that. I had been thinking I missed the way he touched me—the way he fucked me—and I'd wanted it too damn badly to say no.

I could have at least been wise enough to leave after he fell asleep or woke up before the sun rose in the sky. Because I wasn't sure I was ready to face what I had done last night. More importantly, I wasn't ready to face *him*.

If I saw any sign of remorse on his handsome face, I just might lose it.

All throughout our relationship, Preston had always been affectionate with me. He always held my hand and put his arm around me in public. He loved being close when we curled up to watch movies at home. And I never questioned his attraction to me. When it came to sex, he couldn't keep his hands off of me, even after years of marriage.

After Paxton was born, in the beginning, Preston was still his usual loving self, and for a while, he got more doting while I recovered from my C-section. He was especially attentive when it felt like I was constantly breastfeeding Paxton. I didn't think much of it until after I went to my OB/GYN and got the all clear to have sex again, and Preston turned me down.

At the time, he was working full-time, and we had a baby at home, so I figured he was exhausted. I knew I was tired, so it made sense he was too. But Paxton eventually got on a sleep schedule, and when I went back to work, we hired Madison as our part-time nanny, which really helped us out. But even after that, every time I tried to initiate intimacy, Preston always had one reason or another as to why he wasn't in the mood.

He would tell me he had been tired lately, or he was just busy at work, or any number of other excuses. But a woman could only be fed bullshit so many times before she knew something was wrong. I was no exception. But every time I brought it up, Preston tried to reassure me everything was fine even though I knew deep down that it wasn't. And soon, he stopped touching me altogether. Even in a nonsexual way.

Wanting to understand what had happened between us, I ran through every scenario I could think of. I considered that maybe he was jealous about my judgeship. But I had been granted that before Paxton was born, and Preston had been nothing but proud of me. Being a lawyer, I had heard many stories and even painfully considered that Preston was cheating on me with our nanny. But the nanny cams I had installed for child safety showed that not to be even remotely true. When I ruled out every other reason I could think of—from wondering if he secretly wanted me to give up my career to be a stay-at-home mom to if he had erectile dysfunction—I came to the conclusion that it was me.

My husband was no longer attracted to me. He no longer loved me.

Unfortunately, every time I asked him, he told me he was, but it wasn't long before that felt like a lie. Because nothing had changed in or out of the bedroom. I gave him until our son turned six months old. Paxton was sleeping well, we had settled into a normal routine at home, and we were no longer parents of a newborn, struggling with the ins and outs of parenthood. So, when the time came and I was rejected by Preston once again, I knew I'd had enough. I couldn't live with a man who didn't love me and no longer desired me.

But the final straw was when I accidentally found out he had scheduled a vasectomy without saying a single word to me. He hadn't discussed it with me. He hadn't even told me he was thinking about it. And before Paxton had been born, we'd always talked about having more than one child.

Preston had never hidden things from me before, and with us not sleeping together, we were basically room-mates. Roommates who barely even talked to each other anymore. I was miserably unhappy. And since I didn't want a roommate for a husband, I left.

I wasn't going to stay and beg him to love me. I deserved better than that.

Foolishly, when I moved out, I thought Preston would come after me. That he would fight for me.

Instead, he gave me everything I wanted in the divorce.

That was still a slap in the face. He had wanted out of our marriage so badly that, even as a *lawyer*, he didn't fight me on one single cent. The only thing he had been firm about was joint custody of Paxton.

So, while I had no idea why last night had happened or what had changed, I wasn't going to stick around to find out. I wasn't going to risk getting hurt again by someone who was sure to be full of morning-after regret.

He had already fled from his own bed. It was barely seven in the morning on a Saturday, and I could hear the shower running on the other side of the wall. That was the cue I needed to get out of there before he came back.

Quickly but gently, I moved Paxton away from me and kissed his forehead with a whispered, "I love you, little man," before slipping out of bed.

When I stood, the cold air hitting my skin reminded me that I didn't have a stitch of clothing on, and my eyes immediately went to the corner chair. It was the kind of chair people had in their bedrooms to throw their clothes on, and—wouldn't you know it—there was my skirt, my blouse, my bra, and my underwear. Just like when I used to live there.

Preston had gone downstairs and brought my clothes up. Was it another sign he wanted me to leave as soon as possible, or was he just being nice? Maybe both. Either way, I wasn't sticking around to find out.

My bra was in one piece, as was my skirt, but the crotch of my panties had been torn in two while my shirt was missing a few buttons. I put my skirt on, sans underwear, and shrugged on my bra before going to Preston's T-shirt drawer. Pulling out the first one that was on top, I saw that it was his favorite T-shirt, and I smirked. It served him right after ruining an expensive pair of underwear. Since he might wonder what had happened to his tee, I left my ruined panties for him in the drawer and laughed. It probably wasn't the wisest thing to do, but I wanted him to know it was his own fault I had worn his beloved Linkin Park shirt home. I suppose a fair trade would have been my blouse, but I was pretty sure I could find someone to replace the buttons for cheaper than it would be to buy a new one.

Once I was presentable enough, I couldn't help but kiss my baby boy good-bye again before I went downstairs. I panicked for a moment before realizing my purse was still in the kitchen, where I'd left it last night. When I entered, it seemed like picking up my clothes wasn't the only thing Preston had done that morning because the pot of coffee smelled delicious and was calling my name.

Telling myself I needed to get out of there before my ex was out of the shower and that I could stop at a drive-through on the way home, I snatched up my bag and went back the way I'd come. I reached the door, where I paused to put on my heels, and was outside a few seconds later.

As the door closed behind me, my shoulders slumped. My whole reason for going in the house last night was to ask Preston to switch weekends with me, and I hadn't even gotten around to it. Instead, my going inside had complicated everything.

SEVEN
PRESTON

"Yoo-hoo. Preston dear?"

I sighed and let my head fall back against the couch I was sitting in front of while I played on the floor with Paxton.

Was the sound of one's own mother's voice supposed to grate on one's nerves? I didn't need to actually ask someone to know the answer was no.

"In here," I answered and stood.

I wasn't fast enough though because I looked up as Rebecca St. James walked into the living room, saying, "Preston, you shouldn't be sitting on the floor like that. It's not a gentlemanly thing to do."

Taking a quick glance at Paxton, I made sure he hadn't heard his grandmother berate me for playing with him. And rather than rolling my eyes at her for her remark about me sitting on the floor with my son in the comfort of my house, I said, "Pax, your grandmother is here. Do you want to say hi?"

"No."

I stifled a laugh. *Yeah, me neither, kid.*

My mother gasped.

"I play trucks, Daddy," Paxton explained.

I had to fight back the grin that threatened to show itself at my mother's horrified face.

"Well, I never..."

"Mom, he's not even three yet." I already knew she was thinking something along the lines of how my son wasn't acting appropriately.

But as someone who'd grown up hearing how I was supposed to be and how I was supposed to act my whole life, it wasn't something I wanted for Paxton at all. He was a kid and only young once. He had his whole life to conform to society's standards. If he even wanted to. I wasn't putting any of the pressures my own family had put on me on him.

"Preston, it's never too early to start teaching him—"

I put my hand up.

Since my divorce, my patience for my mother had worn thin. Until I'd become a part of Delaney's family, I hadn't known what it was like to be part of a family that was loving and welcoming. Being married to her had helped balance out spending time with my mother, and without them, it made me less tolerant of my mom and her bullshit.

I thought my mother sensed the change in me because she wisely shut her mouth. But she couldn't stay quiet for long.

"Preston, that isn't what you're wearing tonight, is it?"

I sighed again. "No. I am putting Pax to bed before I leave, and then I plan to change."

I was wearing a T-shirt and jeans. I thought most people would just assume I wasn't wearing it out on a date. Although I was very tempted. The woman I was going out with tonight was the daughter of one of my mother's friends. I couldn't imagine she was going to be much fun to be around. And after last night, it was taking everything in me to muster up the energy to go on a date tonight. The only reason I wasn't canceling was because it wouldn't be fair to my date and because it would avoid a fight with my mother if I went.

But the woman I was going on a date with wasn't the person I was thinking about. And she definitely wasn't the one I wanted to be with.

I shifted away from my mother so I could adjust my sudden erection in my pants. Just the mere thought of fucking my ex-wife last night had me hard. I'd been trying to not think about her all day, but it had been a struggle, which meant I'd been uncomfortable most of the day. Not that I understood how. I had come in Delaney three times last night. At thirty-eight, I no longer had the stamina I'd had when I was eighteen. Except for maybe when I was around her, it seemed.

"Well, are you going to get ready?"

I groaned. My mother's voice was like nails on a chalkboard, but at least it was exactly what I needed to get rid of my hard-on.

"Yes, Mother."

"No need to get—"

"Come on, Pax. It's time to brush your teeth and go to bed."

He looked up at me, and I wondered if he was going to be difficult, like he had been last night in the bathtub.

But he said, "Okay," and put his trucks in his toy box.

"I'll be back," I told my mom. "I'm going to put him to bed and change."

"Take your time."

Paxton grabbed my hand. "Hi, Gamma," he said, finally acknowledging her.

"Hello, Paxton," she said with a bit of disdain that she was not good at hiding.

She was still bothered by the fact that we hadn't named him Preston Charles St. James IV, but Delaney had been adamant before we even got married that she didn't want to name any of her children the same as someone else in the family. I didn't argue because I had never liked being the third.

And with so many things being electronic, I had already seen what happened with sharing a name. My father and I were mixed up all the time. It still happened occasionally even though he had passed away. In the end, I was happy to name our son Paxton Charles. He still got part of his family name but part of his own too. We'd even chosen a similar name to Preston, but my mother wasn't happy with Paxton.

But at this point in my life, I didn't really care. Delaney and I weren't changing his name.

"Let's go, buddy."

I took my son upstairs, brushed his teeth, and put him to bed. Then, I forced myself to my bedroom to change clothes when I would rather go to bed. I had not slept enough last night, and I had gotten up way too early when Paxton crawled into my bed.

I was used to him doing that most mornings, but there had been less room with his mother on the other side, and I hadn't been able to go back to sleep. Paxton was the cutest bed hog, but he was still a bed hog.

I was still a little perturbed that Delaney had snuck out while I was in the shower, especially since I had tried to be nice by bringing her clothes upstairs and starting coffee for her. But on the other hand, I understood why she'd crept out before she had to see me. I hadn't been the best husband at the end of our marriage.

Unfortunately, I couldn't change the past. I could only move forward.

And I supposed, even if I was tired, staying up half the night to be inside my ex-wife had been worth it.

I pulled out a pair of black pants and a dark green button-up shirt from my closet and got ready for my date.

As I checked my appearance in the mirror, I was sure my mom would say something about me missing a tie, but things were different from when my mother and father had dated. Also, I wore a tie to work every day. If I could skip it on my days off, I was going to.

I still had a couple of minutes before I had to leave, but since I didn't want to make small talk with my mother, I decided to leave early.

"Mom, I'm taking off," I said as I walked through the kitchen to the door leading to the garage.

She looked up from her thick leather planner when I entered, but before she could make any remarks on my outfit, I continued, "Paxton is sleeping. He should stay that way. I made sure he didn't nap too long this afternoon. But if he wakes up, you can call me."

She put a hand on her hip. "Preston, I have raised a child. I'm sure I can handle putting him back to sleep."

I held in a snort. My nanny had raised me. I could probably count on two hands the number of times my mother had read me a bedtime story.

While I appreciated Paxton's nanny, Madison, especially when it came to sharing custody with Delaney, I had been adamant that she wouldn't live with us. I wanted her to go to her own home each night because I didn't want her raising our son. She was his caregiver, not his parent.

"I'm sure you can," I said. "But if you need me, I'll have my phone on."

She pursed her lips. "We'll be fine." A smile replaced her frown. "Besides, I want you to enjoy yourself tonight."

"I'll try," I muttered and walked out the door.

But when I got to the restaurant and met my date, it confirmed what I'd already suspected. Anna seemed like a perfectly nice lady, but she wasn't the one I wanted.

EIGHT

DELANEY

I TRIED NOT TO NOD OFF AS I LISTENED TO MY DATE, Clint, drone on and on about his job as a tech engineer. I was sure he found his career interesting, but unfortunately, I did not.

To be honest, I didn't find anything about him interesting. I had completely forgotten I was even supposed to go to dinner that night until my friend messaged me with a reminder this afternoon. And since said friend was the mayor of Minneapolis, I couldn't possibly tell her that I wanted to cancel because I had slept with my ex-husband the night before. Nadine and I weren't that close, and I had zero desire or need to involve her in my sex life. She also had a lot of power in the city, and I didn't need to risk getting on her bad side.

So, I'd gritted my teeth and met her husband's cousin with a fake smile as I counted down the minutes until I could go home, put on my most comfortable pajamas, and go to bed.

I felt like a bitch, but didn't this dude do anything for fun? Didn't he have any hobbies he could tell me about? We hadn't even ordered our food yet, and I already wanted this evening to be over.

Just when I thought the night couldn't get any worse, movement toward the front of the restaurant caught my eye. I stopped breathing and did a double take in disbelief. It was Preston. He was with a beautiful and elegant woman, and they were being seated at a table for two.

Trying to not let it bother me since I was on my own date, I looked away. But the pinch in my chest was back, and I couldn't stop my eyes from finding him again.

I thought back to Vivian's St. Patrick's Day party when my ex had dropped by. He'd left soon after, saying he had other plans. Was this the person he'd had other plans with that night? How often did they see each other? Had I had sex with Preston while he was seeing someone else?

I didn't realize I was still staring in his direction until he turned his head toward the back of the restaurant. Quickly, I lifted my menu up from where it had been sitting open in front of me.

Shit. I really hoped he hadn't seen me.

I didn't know what the chances were that the two of us would be on dates at the same restaurant the night after we slept together. I must have done something to piss off fate because I couldn't believe this was my life.

"Did you need something?"

Turning back to Clint, I furrowed my brow. "What?"

"You were looking off into the distance, and now, you're really staring at your menu. Do you have a question for our server?"

Chuckling, I shook my head. I didn't have a question for our server, but it wasn't a bad idea to try and get her attention. The sooner we ordered our food, the sooner we'd get it, and the sooner we'd eat and this whole night would be over.

"I guess I was wondering when she was coming to take our order."

"They seem busy tonight."

Not busy enough that Preston had gone somewhere else to eat.

"Yes, I'm sure she'll come back soon."

"Anyway, what was I talking about?"

"I..." Had no idea.

"Never mind." My date smiled, waving his hand in front of him. "I remember."

That was a relief because I sure didn't, and I felt bad for not paying closer attention.

Checking to see if Preston was facing away from me, I put my menu back down.

I was still fighting to listen to the conversation without a single sighting of our server when my phone vibrated in my purse a few minutes later. And even though I knew it was rude, I snuck my cell out and onto my lap.

My eyes widened when I caught a glance at the person who'd texted me.

> **Preston:** I can't stop thinking about how good your pussy tasted last night.

With a quick flip of my phone, I turned it down, as if everyone around me could read the words on my screen.

Jesus. I hadn't heard from him all day, and he'd sent this to me without any warning. While we were both on dates.

I shifted in my seat at the sharp flare of desire inside me and messaged him back.

> **Me:** Does your date know you're sending dirty texts to another woman while you're out with her?

I watched from the back of the restaurant as Preston stiffened, and I bit back my laugh. So, he hadn't caught me watching him earlier when he walked in.

With some miraculous stealth, he managed to scan the room without making it too obvious he was searching for someone or something. He grinned when he found me and shook his head. His eyes went to my date next, and he frowned before turning back around.

He sent another message.

> **Preston:** You wanted to ask me something last night, but didn't get around to it. Ask me now. I'll say yes if you let me eat your pussy again.

I closed my eyes for a moment and swallowed. Why

did my ex have to be one of the few men I'd dated who liked to go down on me? And why did he have to be so good at it too?

Memories of last night came back to me in waves. I knew I should feel guilty for ignoring my date, and I should also disapprove of Preston texting me while he was on his own, but I couldn't do either.

I liked what had happened between us too much. And I didn't want to admit it, but I wanted him to myself.

But I couldn't give in to him just like that.

> Me: You don't even know what I'm going to ask you.

> Preston: I don't care as long as I get to feast on your delicious cunt.

My cheeks heated. I was used to my ex-husband's dirty talk and texts, but it had been a long time since I'd been on the receiving end of them. And I had certainly never had to read stuff like this when I was sitting across from another man and Preston was sitting across from another woman.

> Me: What if it's a huge favor?

> Preston: The longer you wait to ask, the hungrier I get.

I rubbed my thighs together under my skirt and tried to calm my libido.

> **Me:** I need ten thousand dollars.

I smiled and hit Send, thinking he'd tell me there was no way in hell he'd loan me that much money.

> **Preston:** Cash or check?

No way. I couldn't believe it. If I'd asked him that question two days ago, he would have laughed at me.

> **Preston:** Joke's on you because I would give you a hundred thousand.

My mouth dropped open at the word *give.* Not loan. *Give.*

Okay, he had to know I was joking with him, and he was giving it back to me. That had to be why he was saying yes.

> **Me:** I know you're kidding. You wouldn't just give me that much money.

> **Preston:** Who's kidding? I'm absolutely serious. When do you need it by?

He's serious?

Full of shock, I almost forgot I was on a date, and I knew now was not the time for this.

> **Me:** I don't really need money. I was just messing with you.

> Me: Please don't worry about what I was going to ask you last night.

> Preston: I can't help it. You don't seem to understand how much I want you.

Fuck me. I swallowed and put the back of my hand to my hot cheek.

He needed to stop torturing me.

> Me: You don't need me. You have a perfectly lovely woman sitting across from you. I'm sure she would be happy to let you go down on her.

I needed to put an end to this.

> Me: You should take her home and do that. And maybe I'll take my date home and let him do it to me.

I hesitated before sending the last message because even picturing Preston with that other woman for a single second made me sick. And there was no way I was letting Clint anywhere near me.

But I wasn't sure what kind of game Preston was playing. Was he flirting with me as foreplay before he took the other woman home? After all, he had brought her on a date, not me. Maybe after being with me for over ten years, he'd realized how much he'd missed sleeping around. Maybe he wanted both of us, and one woman was no longer enough for him. Or maybe it was the chase he missed. Maybe he only wanted me because he didn't have me anymore.

Knowing I didn't want to stick around to find out his response, I hit Send and shoved myself up from my chair.

Clint sat back, eyes going wide. "What's wrong?"

"I need a minute," I said, shoving my phone in my purse, which hung on the chair.

I didn't want to see what Preston said back to me. I didn't want to hear about him with someone else, nor did I want him to flirt with me when he wasn't mine anymore.

I spun around and headed toward the restrooms. I just needed to get my head on straight.

NINE
PRESTON

Delaney flew by my table without a single glance in my direction.

Rising from my chair, I told the woman my mother had set me up with, "I apologize. I need to use the restroom."

Anna blinked at my sudden announcement but smiled and said, "Okay."

We'd been making polite conversation since we'd arrived, and it was apparent she wasn't into me any more than I was into her.

Of course, she probably wasn't messaging her ex under the table, telling him she wanted to go down on him, and I felt terrible about that. But being on a date with another female reminded me how much I only wanted one woman. And it wasn't Anna.

I caught up to Delaney right as she reached the women's restroom, and I pushed the door open over her head.

Spinning around, she gasped. "What are you—"

I shoved her inside and flipped the lock behind us as I hauled her body to mine. "What's with the last message, Delaney?" Walking us toward the sink, I stopped when we reached the counter.

She stared back.

I wrapped my hand around the front of her throat. "Answer me."

She swallowed under my palm. "You're on a date. I don't know if this is some kind of weird foreplay you're doing before you take her home and—"

I spun her round to face the mirror and placed her hands on each side of the glass. Running my hand up her leg, I nuzzled her neck as I watched her reaction. "I don't think you understand me. I don't want her. I want you, Laney."

She closed her eyes, and her mouth fell open as she took in more air.

I grazed the inside of her thighs and paused when I reached the top. "Delaney," I whispered in her ear.

Her lids fluttered open.

"I'm only here with her so my mother will stop bothering me. I don't want to have anything to do with her."

Hooking my fingers in her panties, I tore the crotch away and thumbed her piercing. The piercing *I* had given her that she still had in her body. Even though she had probably changed out the jewelry, I had put the piercing there in the first place.

"I want *you*." I sank my fingers in her pussy, and my

59

dick throbbed against her ass at how soaked she was. "You, Delaney."

Pulling out just enough to rub her clit, I smiled when Delaney moaned.

"Fuck," I groaned. "I want to eat you so bad."

Her head fell back against my chest, eyes closed again.

"Tell me you want that too. Tell me you want me more than that putz out there."

She licked her lips. "Nadine set me up." Deep breath. "I didn't want to come. I'd forgotten all about tonight, but it felt like a bad idea—" She bit her lip as I pushed inside her again and found her G-spot. "It felt like a bad idea to tell the mayor no, especially at the last minute."

"Smart woman." I sucked on her neck. "That means I'm the only one who's going to be fucking you tonight. Now, tell me what I want to hear, baby."

She shook her head.

"It's okay," I reassured her. "Tell me."

Her breath hitched. "I want that too."

"Want what? Say it?"

"I want you to eat my pussy."

I nipped her shoulder. "Yeah, Laney, I know you do."

Unfortunately, we were in a restroom and didn't have as much time as I wanted to take with her before someone might need to come into the bathroom.

I flipped her dress up and unbuttoned my pants.

"I promise to take my sweet time between your legs later." Fisting my cock, I rubbed the head between her drenched slit. "But for now, I'm going to fuck you." I drove inside her, and her hips bucked. "Hold on, baby."

Wrapping an arm around her waist, I thrust into her, riding her hard. She hitched her ass up, changing the angle of my dick so it hit her G-spot. I'd been fucking this woman for years, and she knew how to work my body as much as I knew how to work hers.

With each drive inside her, she grew wetter and wetter, and I put my hand between her legs again to strum her clit the way she loved.

"Laney, I want you to open your eyes and look at me."

She blinked them open and met mine in the mirror.

"You're coming home with me tonight."

She reluctantly nodded.

"Say it," I demanded.

"Yes."

"But first, I'm going to come in you. I want cum leaking out of you as you finish your date. I want to know part of me is inside you while I have to watch you with another man." I put my mouth to her ear. "That way, if you change your mind and let him eat your beautiful cunt, he'll taste me and know I was here first."

Delaney's core clenched around my shaft. "And what if *you* change your mind?"

"Then, you'd better come all over my cock and cover me with your scent so she gets a mouthful of you when she takes me in her mouth."

Her pussy squeezed me again, and I chuckled.

"Fuck. My little slut likes the idea of someone eating

my cum out of her and watching her juices be sucked off me by another woman, doesn't she?"

Delaney shook her head, but I knew it was the idea of it that turned her on. The walls of her cunt were gripping me so tight, and that part of her body didn't lie. She was an exhibitionist at heart, and I always loved indulging her in her fantasies.

Speaking of which...

"You'd better hurry up and come, Delaney. Someone's going to knock on this door any minute. And I think I locked it, but I'm not sure," I lied. "Someone could catch us in here."

She whimpered.

"What would they think, seeing Judge St. James getting her pussy pounded in a public restroom? Do you think they'd watch my cock sink in and out of your pussy, covered in your desire, or would they go tell management to kick us out?"

As if on cue, the door rattled as someone tried to open it.

I clamped a hand around her mouth and yanked her back to my chest. "Come on, Delaney. Come on my cock like the slut you are so I can fill up your pussy."

She screamed against my hand as I bit her neck, and her body shook with the force of her orgasm as I slammed home, exploding deep inside her.

We were breathing hard as the door stopped moving and footsteps walked away.

I hated to cut the moment short, but I quickly pulled out my shaft and stuffed it into my pants.

I pulled the bottom of Delaney's dress down as she leaned over the counter, and I smoothed it out.

"Laney, we'd better get out of here."

She nodded and slowly stood.

I flipped the lock and opened the door as she finished checking over her appearance in the mirror. Grabbing her hand, I drew her out into the hall and against the opposite wall just as a woman and an employee came around the corner.

"Did you see someone come out of there?" the lady asked Delaney and me.

The employee knocked on the door and pushed on the thick wood.

I shook my head. "We just got here."

"It's open." The employee looked annoyed for having to come to the restroom when there didn't seem to be a problem.

"I swear it was locked."

"It's not now," the restaurant worker said and walked away.

The woman looked like she wanted to say more, but she went into the bathroom instead.

"That was close," Delaney said.

"It was." I met her eyes. "But you can't tell me you didn't love it."

She straightened. "Preston—"

I pushed her hair behind her ear and brought the ends

down to cover the bite mark I'd left. "Be careful with that," I said, rubbing my finger over it.

She sighed. "You just had to, didn't you?" She sounded irritated, and I couldn't help but grin.

"You drive me crazy." Picking up her hands, I dropped my smile. "Now, quickly, please tell me what you came to ask me last night. No strings attached."

"I'm supposed to go to a law conference next weekend. Madison was going to watch Paxton, but with her being out of town, I was going to see if you could switch weekends. I'd cancel, but I'm supposed to present."

My brow furrowed. "Law conference? Where is it?"

"Las Vegas."

"Oh shit. That's already next weekend? I'm supposed to be on a panel there."

"Preston, really?"

I laughed. "Hey, I knew it was coming up, but you know my assistant knows how busy my schedule is. She only tells me what's going on for the week we're trying to get through. I'm sure she'll remind me on Monday."

"You owe her a raise."

"I already gave her one this year."

"Then, an end-of-year bonus."

"I'll think about it." My grin was back because I hadn't been looking forward to the conference in Vegas, but now that I knew Delaney was going, I couldn't wait. But I knew she was in a bind. "Your presentation is more important than me being on a panel. If you need me to cancel, I can stay home with Paxton."

She stopped me with a hand on my chest and shook her head. "No. My sister already offered to take him. And my parents said they would help. I just need to call and make sure it's okay."

"Are you sure?" I really wanted her to say yes.

"I'm sure." She tried to give me a smile, but it didn't quite reach her eyes. "I mean, if we were still married, they'd have to watch him with Madison being gone."

My good mood was suddenly ruined by the reminder that she was no longer my wife, but my ex-wife.

The woman came out of the bathroom and nodded at us before walking away.

As soon as it was clear, I drew Delaney into my arms. "I was serious about you coming home with me tonight."

She nodded. "I know."

"Are you coming?"

She hesitated for a moment, but nodded again. "Yes."

TEN

DELANEY

Preston insisted I park in the garage since I was staying all night, so I pulled into my old spot and followed him inside. I soon realized I should have waited in my car until he got rid of his "babysitter."

"Preston, is that you?" came from the living room when we walked in.

I shuddered. My former mother-in-law's voice was like nails on a chalkboard. And I was mad at myself for not thinking about asking who was watching Paxton while he was on his date.

Spinning around, I was just about to march back into the garage when she entered the kitchen.

"Oh, you brought your date home. Hmm. I don't remember JoAnn's daughter being a brunette."

Slowly, I turned to face my ex's mother.

She gasped. "Delaney? What—why—" She pursed her lips and looked at her son. "Why is she here?"

I rolled my eyes.

Rebecca St. James had never liked me. She also never bothered to hide it. She was the one thing I absolutely did not miss about being married to Preston. She had always been awful toward me and made no qualms about the fact that she thought her son should have married someone more high society.

Preston spread his hand wide and rubbed his temples before dropping it with a large sigh. "Mom, I ran into Delaney at the restaurant. She came to see Paxton."

Rebecca looked at the clock on the oven and back to her son. "It's almost ten o'clock." Her eyes narrowed. "I set you up with a perfectly respectable lady tonight, Preston. One who wouldn't come home with you for relations." Her scornful gaze swung in my direction. "Unlike this harlot—"

"*Enough.*" Preston's voice was firm.

My eyes widened at her blatant rudeness. My ex-mother-in-law might have always made it clear she didn't like me, but she had never called me names before.

Preston glanced my way and gave me a polite smile that had nothing to do with happiness. "Give me a minute."

"Sure. Take your time."

At this point, I was not feeling sexy in the least. As soon as his mom left, I might literally go see Paxton, then escape home. I was pretty immune to Rebecca and her open disdain, but it was still a mood killer.

Preston grabbed his mother's elbow like she was a child. She tried to shake him off, but he directed her to the front of the house at a fast clip, leaving her to follow or possibly lose an arm.

This was new.

He'd never manhandled her before.

As soon as they were out of sight, I sprinted after them. I stopped at the edge of the dining room so they couldn't see me, but I made sure to stay within hearing range. Partly because I was curious and partly because I didn't know if I would have to intervene. But mostly because I was curious.

"I think it's time for you to leave," Preston said.

Rebecca huffed. "I can't believe you did that," she said, completely ignoring what her son had just said to her.

"Me? I can't believe you. You have no right to talk about Delaney like that."

"Did you not bring her home to do something inappropriate?"

"Whatever I brought Delaney home for is none of your fucking business."

I silently gasped. Preston *never* swore in front of his mother, much less when speaking *to* her.

He was pissed.

Rebecca let out a horrified gasp. "Preston Charles—"

"Save it. That woman in there is my wife and the mother of your grandchild, and she deserves respect."

My heart swelled at his words as heavy footsteps pounded across the floor and the front door was opened.

"Now, get out of my house until you can learn to behave yourself." Preston's voice was level but full of bite.

"Well, I cannot believe you are speaking—"

I rolled my eyes. The woman didn't know when to give up.

"Get the fuck out of my house."

Holding my breath, I waited to see if his mother argued again. If she did, I was going in there before Preston blew a blood vessel.

But after several beats, I heard the clicking of the high heels she always wore on the hardwood of the entryway and then the concrete on the front stoop.

"You're going to regret this—"

The door slammed closed.

"I doubt that." He muttered it so low that I almost didn't hear him.

I stepped around the corner just as Preston turned around.

"Are you okay?" I asked.

While I'd loved hearing him give it to his mom because she'd had it coming for years, guilt suddenly descended on me like a rain cloud. She was his only living parent. If I hadn't come to the house tonight, they wouldn't have gotten in a fight.

Preston's jaw ticced from him clenching it so hard, but he didn't answer me.

"I'm sorry."

His eyes narrowed as he glared at me. "Whatever the fuck for?" he bellowed.

I lifted a shoulder. "If I hadn't been here, you wouldn't have fought."

Preston shoved his hands onto his hips and sighed,

some of the anger leaving his body. Shaking his head, he said, "No. She's the one in the wrong. You didn't do anything to deserve her treatment of you. You never have."

Putting one foot in front of the other, I slowly padded closer to Preston. The whole time we'd been together, he had always tried to keep the peace between Rebecca and me, but he'd always been respectful to his mother. Usually, he cut her off before she said anything too bad, and then he would ask her to stop before she could say anything she couldn't take back.

But tonight, he'd told her off, and he'd stood up for me in a way I'd never seen him do before.

And it was probably inappropriate of me, but I was full of desire for my ex-husband. He looked so proud and strong and angry on my behalf. I couldn't help but want him. I was so ready to jump him. It was as if our quickie in the restroom had never happened.

When I reached him, I clutched the front of his shirt. "Preston?" I whispered.

He met my eyes.

"What are we doing here?"

His brow furrowed.

"Last night and now tonight? What are we doing?"

His expression relaxed. "I honestly don't know. I just know...I want you. And right now, I'm too tired to try and figure it out."

I understood exactly what he meant. If he had asked me the same question, I wouldn't have had an answer either. And trying to figure it out sounded exhausting.

Spreading my fingers out on his chest, I said, "I want you too."

A small smile tugged at the corner of his lips. "You do, huh?" His hands finally left his sides and wrapped around me.

"Yeah." I traced his lips. I'd always loved how big they were, and I missed being able to touch them. "Do you think Paxton's still sleeping?" I asked as I slowly pulled Preston toward the stairs behind him.

He snorted. "I've seen that kid get up, still half-asleep, because he's worried he's missing something."

I grinned. "I call it his zombie mode."

"It's fitting."

"It is. And since he's still out, I want to do this." I swung Preston around and pushed him down on the stairs.

"Oof," he said and laughed. "What was that for?"

Reaching under my dress, I pulled off what was left of my thong. It had been nothing but a decoration around my waist for a couple of hours, but I hadn't bothered taking it off.

I let the scrap of fabric dangle on one finger. "You now owe me two pairs of panties. If you keep this up, I'm not going to have anything left to wear."

Preston bit his bottom lip and slowly pulled it out from between his teeth. "I'd tell you I'm sorry, but I'm not." He shrugged. "They were in my way. They had to go."

"And for that, you're going to be punished."

He smirked. "How so?"

Sashaying closer, I put one foot on the step next to his

head. I was just about to lift my dress to show him what he was missing but dropped it at the last second.

But my move still worked the way I wanted because his eyes glazed over as I bent my knee and pushed my crotch to his face. He inhaled, and just as he reached for my ass, I stepped back and shook my finger.

"Oh, no. No dessert for you."

He groaned and dropped his head forward. When he lifted his chin, he gave me his best puppy-dog eyes. "Baby, please. I promise I'll make it good for you."

I moved close again and cupped his chin. "Oh, of that I have no doubt."

His eyebrows rose expectantly.

"But I think I should be the one to eat first."

I slowly lowered myself to my knees and pushed his legs apart as his breath hissed. His eyes on me, he tracked my every movement as I reached for his pants, unfastened them, and pulled out his beautiful cock.

I sucked in a breath and shivered.

His lips weren't the only thing I'd missed touching.

Gripping him, I kissed his base between where my thumb and fingers couldn't close around his girth and sucked on the taut skin.

"Fuck, Laney," he whispered over me.

I placed open-mouthed kisses up until I reached the top, where I switched hands and started at the base on the opposite half. When I reached the head, I twirled my tongue around the tip and sucked it into my mouth, then down, down to the back of my throat.

I had worked years to get all of Preston's dick in my mouth, and I was very happy to see that I hadn't lost the skill.

I swallowed on the tip, knowing it would drive him crazy, and was rewarded with a large curse. Then, he was dragging my mouth up and off of him.

His breathing was ragged as he stared at me.

"What's wrong?" I asked with a grin, knowing full well he was too close to coming when he wasn't ready.

Getting to my feet, I stepped on each side of his legs.

This time, when he grabbed my ass, I let him. Shoving his nose between my legs over my dress, he breathed in deep and growled. He looked up at me and lifted one large hand to cup the back of my neck.

"I haven't had my dick sucked since before Paxton was born, and there is no way I'm going to last."

I had to hide my surprise. When I'd gotten pregnant with Paxton, I had also gained a strong gag reflex, to the point that I could barely brush my teeth, so I had stopped giving Preston blow jobs. Which meant no one had given him head since me.

A sudden warmth went through my body. "Fuck me, Preston," I whispered.

His other hand went under my dress to my bare butt cheek, and he used both to draw me down to his lap. I reached underneath and grabbed his cock, lining my pussy up over him.

He yanked me down, and with one smooth thrust, he was inside me. And in this position, I felt so full of him, more than I had earlier tonight and the night before, and I gently shifted my hips.

"I know what we're doing here, Delaney."

I stopped and lifted my gaze to his face. "What?"

"We're fucking."

Tightening my core around his shaft, I said, "I think that is obvious."

He squeezed my ass. "That's not what I meant."

"Okay, what did you mean?"

"I don't want to fuck anyone else but you, Delaney, and I know you don't want to fuck anyone else but me."

"I never said that."

"You didn't have to. Your fucking cunt did." He shoved his hips up, and I moaned. "But you're welcome to tell me I'm wrong."

All I could do was shake my head because he was right. Wanting to have sex with anyone else but this man wasn't even a thought that had crossed my mind. No one made me come like him.

"Then, how about we make a little arrangement between the two of us?"

"What kind of arrangement?"

He pulled my head down until our lips almost touched. "We fuck no one but each other. You want to get laid? You call *me*. And *I* will call you."

It was what I wanted, but part of me was scared. "Why?"

"Because your pussy is the only one I want," he growled. "And I want to be the only one to touch it."

Slamming his lips over mine, he nudged my mouth open with his tongue. He licked his way inside, taking his time until I was moaning and rotating my hips over his.

He drew slightly away. "Is that a yes, Laney?"

I nodded. "Yes."

"Thank fuck." He smiled and leaned back, his eyes heating. "Now, ride me until you come."

ELEVEN
PRESTON

I ROLLED OVER IN BED WITH A GROAN, MY ACHES AND pain reminding me I was going to be thirty-nine soon. Getting old was a bitch on the body, and staying up two nights in a row to have sex with Delaney had everything in me protesting.

Slowly, I lifted one lid to peek around the room, and in the predawn light, my gaze immediately landed on my gorgeous ex-wife lying next to me in bed.

One of her arms was thrown over her head, and the other was on her stomach. Her mouth was slightly open as her chest rose and fell with her deep breaths. But the best part was how the covers were down around her waist, revealing her pink nipples, peaked from the cool morning air.

I adjusted the sheet around me and ran a thumb underneath one tip, taking in the changes breastfeeding had done to them. When we'd been married, she'd been worried about how big her areolas were getting and if her boobs would sag after she was finished nursing Paxton. I noticed they weren't quite as perky, but I thought everything about her body was beautiful. All the changes her body had gone through for the little human we'd made, who was sleeping down the hall, were extraordinary.

But the changes hadn't been worth the price we were almost forced to pay.

As if Delaney could sense my sudden anguish, her eyes blinked open, and she smiled at me. "You okay?"

Seeing her alive and smiling calmed me.

I scooted closer. "Yes."

I missed waking up next to her. I missed going to bed beside her every night. The end of our marriage was a bit of a blur because I'd been dealing with stuff, but I had known she wasn't happy. I regretted how things had ended and that they had ended at all, so I was going to enjoy her being here in my bed and in my life while I could.

She rolled on her side to face me and did a quick glance over my shoulder to check the baby monitor.

I pulled her into my arms. "What about you? You good? Is Pax still sleeping?"

"Yes. I slept great, and it looks like he's still out like a light." Her hand ran around my chest. "What were you thinking about just now?"

"Your incredible body..." And I didn't want to talk about the other thing, so I brought up something else I should have mentioned last night. "I'm sorry my mother is such a bitch. She should have never called you a harlot."

Delaney stifled a laugh. "It's kind of funny today because it's such an old-fashioned term."

It was kind of funny, but... "Still, she was basically calling you a slut." I cupped her ass and yanked her core to my dick. "No one gets to call you that but me."

She rubbed herself against me and smirked. "Oh, really?"

"Oh, yeah. She meant it as an insult. I mean it as a term of endearment."

She laughed again. "A term of endearment, huh?"

I smirked. "Something like that." More like I did it because it turned her on. And I loved turning her on.

Delaney grinned. "What if I told you that rumors were flying around your firm that your mother had found a new boyfriend and moved to Cabo, and that's why she no longer lives with you?"

"You're shitting me. How do you know this?"

"Don't tell her I told you this, but Vivian mentioned it one day at lunch."

I chuckled. "My mother would die of embarrassment if she knew that people thought she got a boyfriend and moved to Cabo. She would *never* replace my father." Not because she loved him, but because she didn't want anyone to judge her despite the fact that she was a widow and not a divorcée. Apparently, I could get remarried, but she couldn't. She had sexist double stan-dards, even for herself. "What did you tell Vivian?" I asked.

"The truth. That she went on a vacation to Paris with

her high-society friends and that was when the two of you decided it was best she move out."

"I wonder what other rumors there are about me around the office."

"I'm sure there are a few. You are the head honcho after all."

"When we go to Vegas, do you think there will be rumors if you stay with me?"

I had thought about it after she fell asleep last night, and since we'd decided to no longer fight our attraction to each other, spending our nights together while in Vegas made perfect sense.

Her mouth parted in surprise. "Are you sure we should do that?"

Running a finger around her nipple, I said, "You know you're going to be in my hotel bed every night. We might as well stay together. Why have an arrangement if we don't take advantage of it?"

Closing her eyes, she sighed and pushed her chest toward my hand.

I chuckled. "I think that's a yes."

She looked at me and smiled. "It's a maybe."

"Maybe? I don't think so."

"So, I'm supposed to cancel my hotel room? But are you going on Thursday or Friday? Because I was going on Thursday."

"Uh..."

"Oh, that's right. You need to ask your assistant," she teased.

"One moment." I reached behind me to the nightstand to grab my phone. Delaney turned to grab hers while I pulled up my calendar. "Hmm."

"What?"

"It says I'm going on Friday afternoon, but she also has that the conference starts on...Thursday, is it?"

"Thursday evening is just a meet and greet. Friday morning is when everything really starts."

I frowned for a moment until I realized why my assistant had me going on Friday afternoon. "I understand why she did it. I'm not on the panel until Saturday, and I have Pax until Friday morning." I looked up from my phone to Delaney. "I also didn't really want to be there for any longer than I had to until now."

She ran her heel up my calf. "I'll ask Natalie if she can take Paxton one more night. If she can't do it, my parents can. Then, you can go with me on Thursday. I'll forward my confirmation email so you can try to get there around the same time as me."

I threw my phone behind me on my pillow and rolled us over. "Are you sure?" I sucked one of her berry tips into my mouth.

"Yes," she said with a hiss. "She already texted me this morning, asking about my trip. She's probably up with the baby. Should I text her?"

Releasing her nipple, I kissed my way over to the other breast and gave it the same attention before I pulled away and gazed at Delaney. "Call her."

Her eyebrows arched. "Call? Now?"

"Yes. If she's okay with it, I need to let my assistant know to change my plane ticket right away."

Actually, I was going to change my ticket and Delaney's so we could fly together. My assistant was good, but in light of the gossip going around the office, it was best not to tempt her with information she might want to spread.

"But I thought..."

"Thought what?" I asked with a smirk. I kissed my way down her chest and to her stomach.

"I thought we were going to have sex before Paxton woke up. We probably don't have much time."

Shifting lower on the bed, I lifted one of her knees. "That's why we're going to multitask." I opened her legs wider for me. "I'm going to eat your pussy while you call your sister." I ran a knuckle through her wetness. "I didn't get to go down on you again last night, and I don't know when I'll have another chance before our trip. Thursday seems too far away."

"I—I can't do that," was what she said, but the flush in her cheeks told me she loved the idea.

"Sure you can. And you're going to keep her on the phone until you come. If you hang up"—I shook my head—"no orgasm for you."

"If Natalie finds out about this, she's going to kill me."

Grinning—because that was pretty much a yes—I kissed the top of her cleft. "Then, you had better not let her find out."

Delaney's breathing deepened, and her smell grew

muskier. She was excited about not getting caught while on the phone with her sister.

"Call her," I urged as I threw the sheet over my head and blew cool air on her lips.

Rather than hearing an answer from her, I heard some buttons being pressed, followed by the faint sound of a voice through the phone.

"Hey, Natalie."

Knowing the phone call was probably going to be short, I went right for her sweet spot, swiping my tongue over her clit.

She sucked in a breath and bit her lip. Pulling herself together, she managed to say with an even voice, "I was calling to see if you could still watch Paxton next weekend."

Swirling my tongue around the little nub, I grinned as she gripped the sheet in her hand.

"No, no, he didn't refuse." She paused for a second. "He has to go out of town for something too."

I frowned at this. Did her sister think I would say no simply out of spite?

Or maybe I was assuming things.

I could hear a buzz when Natalie talked, but I couldn't make out what she was saying.

Either way, it was something to worry about later. Right now, I had a pussy I needed to eat.

I took my time, tasting every inch of her as she asked her sister about next weekend. Sometimes, I backed off a little so she could reply to her sister, but other times, I loved to hear her breath catch as she tried to talk in a normal voice.

I sucked her clit along with her piercing in my mouth, then rubbed my tongue under her nub until she was bucking her hips.

Sensing she was right on the edge, I decided to be nice. "Go ahead and hang up, baby. Then, I want you to come all over my tongue."

"Gotta-go-I'll-call-you-later," she rambled into the phone, hit End, and let her hand fall to the side as she arched her hips, riding my face from below, and exploded.

I continued to suck, knowing she would tell me when it became too much for her, and a few seconds later, she closed her legs on my head and twisted her body.

With a little reluctance, I released her little nub and withdrew my mouth. I blew on it again, grinning when she flinched, and then I threw the sheet off my head.

My smile immediately slid off my face as I stared down at Delaney's pussy.

I did a quick check of her face to see if she was watching me, but her eyes were still closed as she lay there, sated. I went back to studying the sight before me.

My sheets were navy blue, and while I'd been eating her out, the sun had risen farther in the sky. When I'd put myself between her thighs, I'd been able to make out shapes, but now, I could see more than the outline of objects.

And right before me, resting on Delaney's clit, was the piercing I'd had made especially for her.

I had always liked what the North Star symbolized—inspiration, hope, guidance—so much so that I always wore a necklace under my clothes and only took it off to sleep and shower.

When we'd gotten Delaney's hood pierced, we'd gone with a green piercing to symbolize my May birthday. But since I'd put her name on my side with pride, I'd wanted something more than just a piercing anyone could buy. So, I'd had one specially made with the North Star on it. Not only to symbolize inspiration, hope, and guidance in our relationship, but to also show that this fucking pussy was mine.

I'd thought for sure she would change it out after our divorce. I'd gone with her to the tattoo shop before, and it'd taken literally less than ten minutes for the piercer to switch it out.

Actually, until Friday night, I had been sure she'd taken it out completely since her piercing had represented our relationship.

But I was wrong on both counts because the curved barbell I'd had made for her lay inches from my face and was still attached to Delaney's body.

"Delaney?"

"Hmm?" she sighed with contentment and opened her eyes. She smiled down at me. "Yeah?"

"You're still wearing the jewelry I got just for you. My North Star."

Eyes rounding as her smile died, she scrambled to sit up, pushing me away. "It doesn't mean anything."

That was what she had said the other night, but that was bullshit.

I frowned and rolled onto my elbows. "The fuck it doesn't."

Shoving out of bed to dart around the room, she stopped when she found her dress. "I think I hear Pax. I'm going to go to him before he catches me in your bed again. I don't want to confuse him any more than we probably already have."

She unlocked the door and ran out before I could say anything else to her. I flopped onto the mattress and checked the baby monitor to see that Paxton was still asleep. He was, and seconds later, Delaney climbed into bed with him.

Rubbing the area over my ribs where I'd gotten her name tattooed on my skin, I knew her words were a lie.

A slow smile curled on my lips.

Her pussy was still fucking mine.

DELANEY

As I snuggled up to Paxton, I was second-guessing getting into this little arrangement with Preston. On the surface, it sounded great. We already knew each other, and I knew he was a good person. We'd already slept with each other, so it wasn't awkward or anything. He knew all my sexual buttons, and it was incredibly nice to not have to train someone new to know my body.

Unfortunately, I had a feeling that no matter how hard I tried to keep my heart from getting broken again, I was doomed to fail.

TWELVE
DELANEY

Thursday, I kept Paxton home with me in the morning. I wanted to give my sister a break since she was going to have him until Sunday when Preston and I got home and because I was going to miss him. Going to an entirely different state was different than having him stay with his father for the weekend. There was something reassuring about knowing he was only staying fifteen minutes away from me even if I didn't see him.

I had just finished packing, and Paxton was helping—in the loosest sense of the word. I was carrying my things downstairs when the doorbell rang.

I frowned and looked at him. "Are you expecting anyone?"

He laughed. "No, Mommy."

I threw my hands up. "Me neither. I guess we'd better see who it is."

In the middle of a weekday, it was most likely a package. I was always ordering stuff and then forgetting I'd ordered it. Sometimes, it was like getting a present from myself.

But when I opened the front door, it was not a delivery.

It was Preston.

And somehow, he looked even sexier in his dark jeans and plain white T-shirt than he had last weekend in his suit. The outfit wasn't the least bit original, but he looked gorgeous.

I groaned inwardly at how easily my hormones gave in when he was around.

He smiled. "Are you almost ready?"

"Daddy!" Paxton barreled past me and launched himself at Preston.

After he caught our son, I held the door open for him to enter.

I patted the top of my large suitcase and kicked my carry-on. "Everything's packed. But what brought you here?"

All week, I'd been questioning whether I'd made the right decision in agreeing to Preston's arrangement. Having him see that I still wore the North Star piercing he had made just for me had left me feeling open and exposed. I had let my guard down, and now, he knew I still cared about him.

Sometimes, I wished that he had cheated on me or something equally awful. It would make it easier to hate him—and I had tried, but I truly couldn't make myself. Having your husband fall out of love with you was pretty awful, but people couldn't control their feelings. I couldn't control not hating him any more than he could control not loving me anymore.

Thankfully, on Sunday, after Paxton woke up, Preston hadn't said another word to me about the situation. He also hadn't acted any differently than normal, and I was grateful. But he'd always been a gentleman. Just another reason I had always liked him. But even if he pretended like he didn't know, we both knew he did. The fact that he'd discovered my secret lingered in the back of my mind, no matter how hard I tried to forget it.

If only I had changed the piercing. If only I hadn't let Preston go down on me until after I left and changed it. Because it had already occurred to me that I would need to do something about it if we were going to keep sleeping together.

But it was too late now.

Preston had offered to let Paxton stay with me during the beginning of the week since he'd had him last weekend and known I wouldn't see him on my weekend. It also gave Preston more hours to catch up on work at his law firm before being out of town for four days. It also made it easier for me to take Paxton to and from my sister's while I went to work. While we'd only exchanged a few text messages since I'd left on Sunday, the law conference started tonight, so I knew I was going to have to see him soon. But

I had a plane to catch, and I didn't understand what Preston was doing at my home.

Then, it hit me. He hadn't seen Paxton for four days.

I bumped the heel of my hand on my forehead. "I'm so insensitive. You wanted to say good-bye to Pax."

His brow furrowed, and he chuckled. "I mean, yes." He gave Paxton a squeeze, and our son grinned and threw his arms around Preston's neck. "But I thought we talked about me changing my plans to go to Vegas today."

"I wuv you, Daddy," Paxton announced, oblivious to the fact that his parents were having a conversation.

"I love you too, buddy."

"We did, but I thought we were meeting there," I said.

Preston laughed and shook his head. "No. When I said I was going with you, I meant, I was going *with* you." He tickled Paxton's belly, who giggled, and said, "I changed my plane ticket to your flight and your ticket to a seat next to mine."

"How did you manage that?"

Preston dropped the hand he'd been using to entertain Paxton and lifted an eyebrow. "You sent me your information, including the confirmation email for your flight."

I tsked at my memory—or lack thereof. "Oh, right."

And now, I didn't have a whole plane ride to prepare myself to see my ex tonight. I would have to sit next to him on the plane too.

Maybe it was a good thing I hadn't canceled my hotel room. I didn't plan to change my mind about telling Preston I would stay with him just because I was being a chicken, but something could happen where I wouldn't want to share a room with him any longer. Or worse, Preston wouldn't want to share a room. Maybe I would stay by myself tonight.

Preston swung Paxton around like he was an airplane and slowly brought him in for "a landing," and I bit my lip. He was even sexy while just being a father to our son.

So, maybe I'd go back to my room after we had sex. No point in denying myself now that the door had been opened to us sleeping together again.

But first, we needed to get to Vegas.

"Okay, Paxton, you need to grab your coat and backpack so we can go to Auntie Natalie's house."

"Yaaaaaaaaaay," he yelled as he ran to get his stuff.

I turned to watch him go so I could see him when he was on his way back and make sure he had picked up both of his things, and Preston stepped behind me and splayed his large hand over my lower abdomen.

"You look delicious. Your ass is killing me in those pants."

"They're just leggings." I had dressed for comfort for my flight.

"That shows every curve and dimple." He pulled me back against him. "What I don't see is a panty line."

I turned my head, feeling good now that I knew I had some of my power back. "That's because I'm not wearing any. You keep ripping the crotch out of the ones I have."

He groaned, pushing his hard-on into me. "You are

evil. And yeah, I found your little present that you left in my drawer where I should have found my favorite tee."

"Serves you right." I grinned. "Besides, I didn't know we were even flying together until you got here. I thought we were meeting in Vegas."

"So, you were going to show everyone else your perfect body?"

"I'm not naked, Pres."

"Laney, you might as well be. Those pants hide nothing."

I shrugged because I was not changing clothes. "I have a long sweatshirt I'm going to wear too. You know how cold I get on the plane."

"Good, because I don't want everyone looking at you."

"Well, you should be okay with it because you're going to be the only one who sees me without *any* clothes this weekend."

He groaned and nuzzled my ear, sending shivers down my spine.

His hand dipped south, but he stopped on my lower pelvis. "Are you still wearing my piercing?"

I swallowed, not wanting to answer.

"Please say yes," he whispered. "I am going to be so hard on the whole plane ride, but I don't care as long as you say yes."

I nodded. "Yes," I said in a low voice.

"*Fuck.*"

I had debated on switching it out now that Preston knew, but I thought changing it would only solidify how big of a deal it was. If I didn't do anything with it, I could play it off as it not being very important. But mostly, I didn't want to. I couldn't even pretend. It was the only thing I still had of our loving marriage besides Paxton, and I wasn't ready to let it go.

"When we get to Vegas, the first thing I'm going to do is fuck you so hard," he said in my ear. "Maybe I won't even wait until we get to our room. I'm going to pull your leggings down and take you in the elevator."

Just the idea of it made my skin flush and core clench.

"Got it," Paxton yelled, and Preston stepped to the side of me right before our son appeared.

Paxton held up his jacket and his backpack. "See, Mommy."

"Good job, buddy."

Preston ruffled his hair. "Mommy's right. You did good, bud."

Paxton beamed with pride.

"We'd better get going." I turned to Preston. "You're okay with stopping by my sister's? Otherwise, I can take Pax there and come right back. She's only five minutes away."

So far, I'd been doing drop-off and pickup at my sister's house, even on the nights when Paxton stayed at Preston's. I wasn't going to keep it up forever, but right now, it gave me a chance to see my son every day and keep my sister out of my hair. She was bound to say something to me once she saw my ex again, which was why I hoped Preston would take me up on my offer.

"Nah. Let's all go, and that way, we can head to the airport right away."

"Together it is." I was going to have to get Paxton inside before Natalie figured out we were there and looked out her window. "You heard Daddy. Let's go get in his truck."

THIRTEEN
DELANEY

WE GOT EVERYTHING OUTSIDE, AND I LOCKED UP MY house. While Preston loaded my bags in the back, I buckled Paxton into his car seat.

When we arrived at my sister's, I jumped out as soon as the vehicle was in park. Preston frowned at my rushing.

When I opened the back door to get Paxton, he said, "Delaney, we have plenty of time to check in and get through security."

I gave him a smile. "I know, but I always worry."

His brow crinkled. "Since when?"

Damn him for knowing me so well.

I shrugged. "I don't know." I grabbed Paxton's stuff off the seat next to him. "Come on, buddy. Let's go see your cousins."

"Yay."

"Say bye to Daddy."

Paxton waved and grabbed my hand as he jumped out.

I shut the door, and Preston rolled down his window.

"What? All I get is a wave good-bye?" he protested as Paxton rushed to the front door.

I shrugged. "I guess you're not any fun."

His eyes heated, and he lowered his gaze. "Oh, I'm plenty of fun. Just ask your pussy."

I made a noise between a squeak and a moan. "Not here."

He snickered. "Pax can't hear me." He lifted his chin. "Go. Drop him off, and let's get out of here. Give the brat a hug and a kiss for me."

"Will do."

Rushing after Paxton, I knocked softly in case my niece was taking a nap, and then I opened the door. I was used to walking in when Natalie knew I was coming, but I wasn't expecting her in the entryway, and I jumped.

Natalie laughed.

"You scared me."

"Eh. You're fine."

I ushered Paxton inside and tried to close the door behind me.

Natalie kept her hand on the knob and looked over my shoulder. "Delaney, I told you I could give you a ride to the airport so you don't have to pay for parking. You know Dad would have driven you too."

"I know, but I didn't need you to do even more favors for me."

My sister was already watching my kid for three and a

half days. I didn't need her to load three children in the car and drive me all the way there.

"And Dad would've had to take time off work. Plus, I get in on Sunday evening around dinnertime. This way is just easier."

She gestured toward her driveway. "So, you used a rideshare?"

I glanced over my shoulder. Preston had put his window up, and the sun glared off it, making it hard to see who was behind the wheel.

Just as I was about to tell her a friend was giving me a ride, Paxton ratted me out. "Tat's Daddy's truck."

Natalie's jaw dropped open. "What the fuck, Delaney?"

"Natalie, not in front of Paxton."

I knew he'd probably heard Preston and me swear before, but I was trying to avoid doing it around him until he was a little older and didn't repeat everything adults said.

She looked down at her nephew. "Paxton, don't say the word Auntie Natalie just said."

"Okay." He looked at me and grinned. "What da fut?"

"Nice, Natalie. You just made it forbidden and therefore exciting."

"He'll forget it in a few minutes. Unlike me."

With a sigh, I knelt down. "Give Mommy a hug." I chose to ignore the swearing since she was probably right about Paxton forgetting.

He threw his arms around me.

"I love you."

"Wuv you too."

"Daddy loves you too."

"I know."

I kissed his cheek, laughing as I let him go. "Go find your cousins and play. I'll see you in a couple of days."

"Okay. Bye, Mommy." Paxton took off, leaving me alone with my sister.

Slowly, I stood, knowing I was going to get a lecture.

"When you asked me to watch Paxton an extra day because your ex-husband was going out of town, you didn't tell me it was to the same place you were going." She crossed her arms over her chest. "He *is* going to Vegas too, right? Otherwise, you'd better have a good reason why you're with him right now."

Thank God she didn't know about last weekend.

"Yes, he's also going to the law conference. You know, because he's also a lawyer. After I asked him to trade weekends, I found out he was attending. We didn't plan this trip together." Not really anyway.

She eyed me suspiciously. "Yet you had to ask me to watch Paxton for him."

I couldn't tell her he'd changed his schedule around to go earlier.

"Yeah, because Madison was going to watch him. And it was either you or Preston's mother."

Guilt hit me for lying to my sister, but I knew she would understand me not wanting his mom to babysit. The other night, when Preston was at dinner, was one thing, but over twenty-four hours was another. I didn't trust his mother to feed him or make sure he didn't hurt himself.

Natalie rolled her eyes. "Okay, that makes sense." She pointed a finger at me. "But it still doesn't explain why you're driving to the airport together." She picked up one of my hands as her face went from angry to concerned. "Delaney, I remember all the nights you cried when you thought no one was looking. I don't want you to get hurt again."

"I love you." If only everyone had someone to look out for them like I had my sister. "But I *do* remember what it was like."

"Do you really though? I know how much you loved him, and I also know how charming he can be. He's not a bad guy, but I'm worried he's going to reel you in, and before you know it, he'll have broken your heart all over again."

It was my turn to roll my eyes. "Nat, I am coming up on forty years old in a couple of years. I am not in my twenties anymore. I can't be swayed by a handsome face and romantic words." I put my hand up. "If Preston even tried that," I added before she could say anything about that.

It was mostly the truth. He'd said some dirty, filthy things to me, but none of them were romantic. And I would like to think I could keep my heart separated from my cooch. Something that had been a lot harder to do in my twenties.

"Listen, we're trying to get along for Paxton's sake, and we're both going to the law conference, where we'll be surrounded by a bunch of lawyers all weekend. It's not that big of a deal."

"If you say so. But if you share a room with him, I'm flying down there to kick your ass."

My eyes got wide, and Natalie laughed, misunderstanding my reaction.

Pulling me in for a hug, she said, "I love you too. Now, go and enjoy some kid-free time. And good luck on your presentation."

The airport was busy when we got there, which wasn't unusual for an international airport in the middle of the afternoon. We went to the counter since I was checking a bag. I never bothered trying to pack everything in a carry-on.

"Where are you headed today?" the lady at the counter asked.

"Las Vegas," I answered as we handed over our driver's licenses to get our boarding passes.

"Oh, fun." She looked at our IDs and faces and handed them back to us.

"Thanks," I said, neither of us bothering to explain we were going for work. She was just being polite and didn't really care what we were flying out of town for.

After getting my suitcase on the conveyor belt behind her, she smiled. "Have a wonderful vacation, Mr. and Mrs. St. James."

The comment jolted me a moment, but without a single pause, Preston grabbed my hand and grinned. "Thanks. It's the first time we've gone somewhere alone without the kid."

She smiled back. "I've been there. Enjoy the extra sleep."

"We will." We turned to leave, and Preston leaned over to whisper, "I'd rather fuck you all weekend than get extra sleep." He kissed my knuckles, and we headed toward our next destination. "Let's go and get through security so we can find our gate."

Since the line was long and crowded, I didn't say anything to him about his conversation back at check-in until we had all our stuff in our hands again after going through security.

As we broke away from the crowd and headed toward our gate, Preston grabbed my hand again.

"Why did you let the lady back there think we were still married?"

He shrugged. "It seemed easier than to tell her we're divorced and try to explain that we're going out of town together."

"You could have told her we're going for work at least. You made it sound like it's a vacation." I didn't know why I cared so much, but I did.

He shrugged again. "Yeah, we're going for work, but it *is* also our first time away from Paxton together. It sounds more fun than a work conference."

He made it sound like we were still together and we

just hadn't had time. And going by his casual attitude, I didn't think he realized what he was doing or that a part of me liked hearing him talk like that.

I wasn't mad or upset, but my conversation with my sister tickled the back of my brain. She'd meant well, but now, I was overthinking this weekend and even this whole arrangement. It was supposed to be fun, no strings attached.

At least, that was what I wanted it to be.

I needed a minute to clear my head.

PRESTON

Delaney tried to shake my hand off as she said, "I need to grab a latte before we go to our gate."

Grinning, I pointed behind me. As she turned, I said, "I knew you'd want to stop for coffee. You always do."

It was kind of her thing before we went on a trip.

Her shoulders relaxed when she saw where we were. I hadn't realized how stiff she was before that.

"Preston."

"What?"

She swung back around to me and shook her head with a smile. "You're making this really hard, you know that?"

I chuckled. "Making what hard?"

"Resisting you."

I barked out a laugh. "Resisting me? Why would you

want to resist me?" I pulled her closer and lowered my voice. "If you resist me, then I can't make you come anymore."

She groaned. "You don't play fair."

"How's that?"

"Because you give the best orgasms," she said almost with a whine.

Grinning again, I whispered, "Well, if your pussy didn't taste so good and if you didn't fuck me like a rock star, I probably wouldn't give you so many."

"Ugh." With a shake of her head, she grumbled, "This is what I mean."

"I don't think you should be trying to resist me at all."

"Why not? You didn't have any trouble resisting me."

Since when?

She was still the most beautiful woman in the world to me. There was no way I could ever *not* want her.

Dropping a kiss on her lips, I muttered, "If you were so resistible, then why have I had to fist my cock every night since Sunday?"

Her mouth dropped open.

I let go of her hand and lightly smacked her butt. "Now, go get your drink so we can find our gate."

The line to the well-known coffee shop was long and the space small, so while Delaney waited to put in her order, I stayed off to the side and studied her.

She'd been quiet since we'd dropped Paxton off at her sister's. When I'd asked her if everything was okay, she'd brushed me off with a simple yes.

I had already figured out that Natalie wasn't my biggest fan, which kind of hurt because, at one time, she had been the closest thing I had to a sibling. I'd understood that she would take her sister's side in the divorce, but Delaney had left me.

Delaney and I had struggled after Paxton was born, and I'd been a shell of a husband, but I'd thought we'd work things out eventually and stay together. Truthfully, I had been in my own head so much back then that I was running on auto. And when Delaney had walked out, while I'd been devastated at the time, I'd also thought she was better off without me.

These days, I didn't feel the same, but I couldn't change the past. The best I could do was try to make it up to her.

Natalie probably blamed me for Delaney leaving, so I was going to have to suck it up. I was sure she had said something to Delaney when we dropped Paxton off. I didn't want to put Delaney in a situation where she was unhappy or where she felt like she was torn between the two of us. She'd already been through so much in her life, and I didn't want to be the cause of her stress. I could only hope to show her and her sister that I wasn't the same man I had been two years ago.

Delaney had seemed to be in a little better mood just before she went in for her coffee, but it crossed my mind that I should give her some space. Maybe I was coming on too strongly.

However, when she walked out a few minutes later, smiling around the cup at her lips, I changed my mind.

Fuck giving Delaney space.

If she wanted me to leave her alone, she'd need to tell me. That woman had never held back when we were married. I couldn't imagine she'd start now.

"Better?" I asked when she reached me, taking her hand in mine.

She nodded. "Yeah, I'm ready to enjoy our work-trip-slash-vacation away from Paxton."

FOURTEEN
DELANEY

"Better?" Preston asked and grabbed my hand.

As I had waited for my coffee, I had come to a realization about Preston. He still remembered things I liked and disliked from when we were together, which meant he still cared about me. I wasn't talking about love, but we didn't have to love each other to care about each other. So, if hooking up with my ex-husband made me happy, I shouldn't let my sister get in my head.

I could sleep with some random dude—already had done that and hadn't liked it—or I could sleep with someone who knew me, someone who knew my body, and someone who gave more than two shits about me.

Preston had offered an arrangement that was purely about sex. He'd never said anything about dating or getting back together. And his not correcting the clerk at the check-in counter wasn't something to be alarmed about because he was right. It was easier than trying to explain how we were divorced, but going on a trip together. Something I wouldn't have thought twice about if Natalie hadn't said anything.

So, I was going to chalk it up as an unnecessary concern and leave it at that.

With a smile, I nodded. "Yeah, I'm ready to enjoy our work-trip-slash-vacation away from Paxton."

We continued to the gate, and it wasn't until they started calling sections that I realized Preston had changed my seat to first class.

As I settled in next to the window, I told him, "When you told me you were changing your flight to mine, I thought you'd be flying coach with me."

"I thought you knew. Didn't you get an email?"

"Probably, but I'm so bad about checking my personal one." My work email took up so much of my attention that I often forgot about my personal email. "I can't believe you scored these seats at the last minute."

Preston shuddered. He was tall, and the one time we'd had to fly coach years ago, he'd been miserable the whole time with nowhere to put his legs that was comfortable for him or those who sat next to him. "I have my ways," he said.

I snorted. "Oh, really?"

While his family had money and influence, I doubted they had enough to bump someone off a flight.

He laughed. "Actually, it was easier to move you up here than it was for me to go back there."

"Well, thanks for not leaving me back there."

"Never, Delaney."

He stood and went to the compartment where he had just stored his luggage and pulled out a hoodie, which was unusual because he ran hot.

"Are you cold?" I asked him as he sat back down.

He shook his head, but didn't say anything because the flight attendants started doing their usual spiel.

I'd heard it a thousand times, so I leaned my head back against the seat and closed my eyes, half-listening while I waited for them to finish.

Before I knew it, I was waking up with my head on Preston's shoulder. I didn't sit up right away though. I was still half-asleep and Preston smelled and felt good. His hand rested on my thigh, and at some point, I had wrapped my arms around his like it was my teddy bear. The best part was that he had draped his open zip-up sweatshirt over me like a blanket, so I was nice and warm.

He squeezed my thigh. "You doing okay over there?"

I tilted my head back so I could see his face. He was holding his phone in his other hand.

"I'm good. Are you reading?"

"Yeah."

"Anything good?"

"It's okay. I'd rather be doing something else."

I chuckled. "I'm surprised you didn't get your laptop out to work on something." I knew he'd brought it because he'd had to take it out of his bag at security.

Putting his phone in the back of the seat in front of

him, he said, "I stayed late the last three nights at work. I'm kind of sick of it."

Preston's work ethic was one of the things I'd always admired about him. He was a hard worker without a doubt, or he wouldn't have his own thriving firm. He'd built Benowitz & St. James from the ground up with his partner. But he wasn't a workaholic who never took time to relax or spend time with his family.

He turned in his seat, causing me to sit up. Pulling his one hand from my thigh, he put it behind my head and slid the other under his sweatshirt that was covering me.

"What are you doing?" I asked.

His palm slid up my leg and over my lower abdomen. "All I can think about is how warm you are between your legs and how you're not wearing any underwear." With a gentle tug on the top of my leggings, he said, "I want to feel your pussy."

Casually, I scanned the area from my spot in the window seat. Many passengers were sleeping or otherwise doing their own thing. The cabin lights were off, and while it was daylight, it was cloudy in whatever part of the country we were flying over.

When I looked back at Preston, I smiled and spread my legs.

He yanked my knee over his before he went back to my pants and slipped his hand inside.

He groaned low when he skimmed over my core, and I knew what he'd found.

"I'm already wet," I told him.

"Yeah, baby, I can tell. You like the idea of me playing with your cunt in a plane full of people, don't you?"

I sucked in a breath. There was no point in denying it. While the humiliation I would feel at getting caught scared me, it also excited me. Part of me wanted people to know how naughty we were.

He put his forehead to the side of my head so his mouth was close to my ear. "I'm going to touch you now because I can't wait any longer."

"Yes, please," I said as I snuck my own hand between his legs. I wrapped my palm around his denim-covered cock just as he pushed his fingers inside me.

I had to bite my lip to keep myself from making noise as I bucked my hips. Unlike Preston, I had not masturbated every night this week, and I hadn't had an orgasm since Sunday morning.

"Fuck, Laney, your pussy is on fire. I wish I could put my mouth on you. I want to taste you so bad." He stroked my G-spot and clit with each word that fell from his lips. "What do you think? Do you think anyone would notice if I got down on my knees and ate your delicious cunt? Would they know what I was doing? Would they know you're my slut?"

I whimpered and lifted my hips to ride his hand. "I'm going to come."

"Fuck it," he growled.

Before I knew it, he yanked his hand out of my pants, was on the floor between my legs, and had my leggings down around my knees. My ass was hauled to the edge of the seat, and within ten seconds of Preston sucking my clit in his mouth, I was coming all over his face.

Barely aware I was on a public plane, where anyone could see me since Preston's body was no longer blocking me in from the aisle, I squeezed my eyes shut and gripped the armrests as my orgasm washed over me in wave after wave.

When it slowly waned, he moved his mouth lower and swept his tongue inside my core before I heard the distinct sound of a slurp. Knowing Preston was licking up my juices was almost enough to make me come again, and when he flicked my swollen nub again, a small tremor went through me.

Preston helped me get my pants back up as he slithered out from under his sweatshirt. And with far more grace than I would be able to pull off, he took his seat again beside me as if he hadn't just gone down on me.

Putting a finger under my chin, he leaned over and kissed me, making love to my mouth with his. When he drew back, he said, "I wanted you to know how good you tasted. Best fucking cunt."

I smiled. "How many have you sampled?"

He smiled back. "You know I wasn't a saint in college, babe."

We'd gone to the same college for our undergrad years before we started dating. Back then, Preston had been a slut.

With a laugh, I said, "Oh, I remember, but what about more recent events?"

"I don't want this to disprove my theory, but yours is the only one I've tasted since we started dating."

I blinked a couple of times. "You mean, like, over ten years ago?"

"Yep." He let go of my chin. "I'll be right back. I need to go relieve some pressure in the bathroom. I'm already starting to ache."

I slammed my hand down on his arm.

Knowing how much Preston loved to go down on me, I was in absolute shock that he hadn't given another woman oral sex since we'd gotten divorced. And, holy hell, that made him that much sexier to me. When he said he couldn't get enough of me, he really meant *me*.

"What's wrong?"

Instead of answering, I moved the sweatshirt over to his lap and looked him in the eye as I unzipped his pants. His cock felt huge in my hand as I pulled him from his jeans.

"I want to touch you," I told him. "Let me take care of you, Pres."

Just like me, he answered my request with his body. He leaned back and let his knees fall to the sides but kept his gaze on mine.

I stroked him from root to tip, wanting to feel every inch of his length as I worked him in my fist. After several passes, I slipped my other hand under the sweatshirt and rubbed my thumb over his slit. I was rewarded with pre-cum, and when I took my hand back out, I stuck my wet digit in my mouth.

"Tell me when you're about to come, baby. I want to taste you too," I whispered.

Preston's cock jerked against my palm, and he dug his fingers into my leg. "I can't wait to get to our hotel room. I am going to fuck you so good."

"I know you will. And I can't wait." My core clenched in anticipation. "But right now, I want you to come down my throat."

He squeezed my thigh. "That's it, baby. That's all I needed." He tore his eyes from mine and closed them as he threw his head back. "I'm ready to come down your pretty throat."

Leaning over, I drew the sweatshirt over my head, and Preston held it up so I had room to work.

I kissed the top of Preston's dick and sucked it into the back of my mouth.

He came almost immediately, and I swallowed until he was finished. I squeezed around his base to make sure I got every last drop of him before carefully sitting up.

I wasn't even all the way in my seat when Preston grabbed me and kissed me again.

When he let me go, he said, "Fuck, babe, you are amazing." He shook his head. "Resistible, my ass."

FIFTEEN
PRESTON

Several hours later, Delaney and I arrived at our hotel.

She checked her watch as we got in line to check in. "We still have time to make it to the meet and greet, but it looks like taking a minute to relax is impossible. We're going to have to get ready right away."

Our plane had needed to circle the airport while we waited for the runway to clear, so our flight had landed later than we had originally anticipated.

It was a good thing everything took place in the hotel so we could literally head downstairs once we finished getting ready for tonight.

The group ahead of us finished, and we stepped up.

"Name of reservation, please?" the man behind the counter asked.

Delaney looked at me, and I gestured toward her to go ahead.

She frowned. "St. James." She cleared her throat. "There might be—"

"Found it. First name Delaney in a nonsmoking king. Does that sound right?"

"Uh..."

"Yes," I answered for her.

"And will you also be staying with Ms. St. James?" he asked me with a smile. "Can I get your name?" He moved on to the second question without waiting for an answer to the first.

"Preston St. James." I never bothered with *the third* part unless I had to. It was a pain in the ass sometimes not to have my own name.

There were a few more clicks on the computer.

"I'll have your key cards ready in a moment," the clerk said and stepped away.

I slid closer to Delaney. "Why do you look so confused?"

She shrugged. "I guess, in my head, I thought I was staying with you in *your* room. When you showed up today, I realized I'd forgotten to cancel mine. It's a good thing I didn't, or we wouldn't have a place to stay."

"Did you really forget, or were you keeping it so you could get away from me?"

"I really did forget." She eyed me up and down. "But it did occur to me that I might want to escape you for a while," she joked.

Placing my hand on her hip, I squeezed. "Oh, no,

there's no way you're getting away from me. You're mine for the weekend."

Her eyes heated, and I thought about all the things I wanted to do to her. I was about to suggest we say screw the meet and greet.

She turned my way. "But what if you get sick of me?"

She was still trying to be playful, but I could see the seriousness in her eyes.

Squeezing her side again, I said, "Never."

If only she knew how much I'd missed her every day since she'd left, she wouldn't even suggest that. I wasn't going to waste any time this weekend being apart any more than we had to.

The clerk came back and slid two cards in envelopes to us. "Here you go. You are all checked in, Mr. and Mrs. St James. We hope you enjoy your stay."

We grabbed our stuff to head to the elevator.

"I suppose that's going to keep happening, isn't it?" Delaney asked.

I didn't tell her I kind of liked it. "Yeah. It happens when we have the same last name."

"I could be your sister," she pointed out.

We reached the elevator, and I pushed the button to our floor. "I don't think so."

"Just because we don't look alike doesn't mean we're not siblings."

I chuckled. "I think it has less to do with how we look and more to do with the looks on our faces."

She wrinkled her nose. "And what look is that?"

116

"The one where we want to fuck each other."

When the elevator doors opened, a family of four stepped out, and we got on.

"Two seconds earlier, and those parents would have had to do some explaining to their kids about the new word they'd just learned."

I laughed. "I'm sure they've heard it before."

"Yeah, you're right. Paxton certainly has."

When we reached our floor, we found our room—406. We went to work on unpacking some things, and we started getting ready for the meet and greet.

Delaney found her clothes and went into the bathroom to change while I got dressed in the main room. A few years ago, she wouldn't have gone to another room to put on different clothes, and I tried not to let it dampen my mood.

After I was ready in my dress pants and button-up shirt, I headed out to the balcony to get a good look at the city from several floors up. There was a small metal table and a single chair, but I skipped it to lean against the railing to get a better view.

When she walked out forty minutes later with her hair done, her makeup on, and in a modest yet sexy red dress, I got hard.

Cocking an eyebrow, I said, "Are you sure we don't have time for a quickie?"

She held up her phone. "Yikes. No. It started five minutes ago."

I grinned. I'd been joking, but I loved that she had

checked.

She dropped her arm. "Besides, I already made myself pretty, and I don't want to ruin anything."

I shrugged. "I was only going to make a mess of your pussy, but I understand." I pushed off the balcony railing I'd been leaning against and put an arm around her waist. With a kiss, I said, "And you are always beautiful, no matter what."

She looked up at me. "Thanks, Pres. The same could be said about you."

"I know."

She rolled her eyes. "Let's go."

I followed her into the hotel room, and I locked the sliding glass door. Delaney grabbed a small purse from her suitcase and slipped her phone and key card inside.

It wasn't until we were at the elevator again that I noticed Delaney had on dark nylons, which made her legs look great.

"I suppose since you're wearing nylons, that means you put underwear on."

The doors parted, and she smiled over her shoulder at me as she stepped on. "Wouldn't you like to know?"

There was another couple inside, also dressed up, so I couldn't guarantee that they weren't going to the same place we were.

I stepped inside next to Delaney and whispered in her ear, "Yes, I would."

She just smirked back at me.

I was hard again and in front of strangers who might also be attorneys.

Delaney bit her lip to stifle her laugh when I had to cross my arms in front of me and lean against the wall to hide my erection.

When we reached the lobby and the couple in front of us got off, I snagged her around the waist when she tried to walk off and rubbed my dick against her ass.

"That was just plain mean." I slid a hand under her dress to find thigh-high nylons and her bare cunt. I released her before I did anything else that might get us kicked out of the hotel. "I stand corrected. Knowing I have to wait to see what you look like in nothing but those stockings is meaner."

She peeked out the doors and then turned around to flash me with a grin on her face.

I shook my head in mock disappointment. "You are just plain evil."

Hitting the button to keep the doors from closing, I stepped around her while she laughed her way out of the elevator behind me.

By the time we reached the table to check in and get our name tags, I'd thankfully lost my erection. And while Delaney still looked good enough to eat, my brain was switching to work mode.

"How long does this last again?" I asked in a low voice

as we walked into the large room, filled with a bunch of lawyers mingling around. "I'm suddenly wishing we had found something to eat before we got here."

My stomach growled, as if to prove my point.

"It's two—two and a half hours? I can't remember. But we don't have to stay the whole time. And"—she smiled at me—"they are serving hors d'oeuvres. And if you're still hungry when we leave, we can go find a real meal."

"Oh, thank God."

"I think food gives people something to do so we don't all stand around, awkwardly trying to make conversation."

"In that case, let's go find someone with a tray."

It was in the back of the room—because of course it was. That way, people had to walk past the other attendees to get to it and maybe strike up a conversation. The good thing was, there was a lot to choose from, so maybe we wouldn't have to find food later.

I loaded up my plate while Delaney was still deciding on what she wanted. "I'm going to go snag a table before someone else gets it."

"Okay."

The table was standing level with no chairs. Probably another way to keep people mingling. Guests were less likely to stay in one place if they weren't sitting.

I had just set my plate down when I heard, "St. James, you dick, is that you?"

Grinning, I turned around to see Theo Vanderpool, one of my old classmates from law school. "Hey, asshole," I said as we clasped hands and bumped chests. "I didn't think I'd run into you here."

I'd been to various law conferences over the years, and I had never seen Theo at any of them, even the ones that were closer to his part of the country.

"What are you doing all the way out here?" I asked.

"I could ask the same of you."

"Minnesota's closer than Connecticut," I pointed out even though neither was close.

He held out his arms. "Yeah, but it's Vegas, baby. Work pays for my flight, my hotel, and I get to play the slots."

Shaking my head, I laughed. "Don't you own your own law firm?"

He shrugged. "Yeah, but it doesn't come out of my personal pocket, so I think it's worth it." He crossed his arms and leaned on the table. "It's gotta be the same for you."

"Yeah. I'm on a panel of lawyers who started their own firms."

"Hey, same. Saturday, right?"

I nodded. "We must be on the same one."

Rather than someone giving a presentation about their experience, a panel gave the attorneys in the audience a chance to ask multiple people questions and get varying answers.

Scanning the room, he turned back to me. "So, work is going well, I'm assuming." He softened his voice. "Is it true you got a divorce?"

Talking about my personal life with an old friend

wasn't off-limits, but I didn't really want to discuss my divorce.

"Yeah," was all I said, hoping he wouldn't ask me any more questions about it.

Keeping his tone low, Theo said, "Since we're two single guys in Vegas, maybe you and I can hit up some of the casinos together. But if not, I've already seen a couple of beautiful women here without wedding rings." He leaned closer. "Over at the food table, there is a brunette in this red dress with slamming hips and an ass for days. I can already picture it—"

A cough sputtered from me. I had just taken a bite when I heard Theo obviously describing Delaney.

As if my friend had summoned her, she appeared at the table. "Hey," she said, setting her plate down.

Theo swung her way, crossing one foot over the other while pasting a cocky smirk on his face. "Well, hello there."

Delaney raised her brow with a look that said, *Who is this guy?*

After holding back a laugh, I tried to wipe the smile off my face. "Delaney, this is Theo Vanderpool, an old class-mate of mine from Georgetown. Theo, this is Delaney St. James, my wife."

SIXTEEN

DELANEY

"Ex-wife," I corrected and held out my hand as some of the color left Theo's face.

The man, clearly rattled, composed himself and shook my hand. He shot a look at Preston. "St. James over here didn't mention you were also here."

Preston popped a carrot in his mouth with a grin. "I didn't get a chance to."

My eyes went back and forth between the two men. "I feel like I missed something."

"I was just telling Preston about this bombshell brunette in a red dress, only to find out you're his ex."

I hadn't expected Theo to actually tell me the truth, and I had to laugh. "Ah." I curtsied. "But thank you for the compliment."

Theo slid over to me. "But since you two are no longer together, if you're looking for a little fun while you're in Vegas, we could get out of here later." He tilted his head in

Preston's direction. "Ditch your ex and go somewhere, just the two of us."

I looked at Preston. Was this guy for real, or was he just messing with his friend?

Preston's jaw ticced, but only for a moment. "Theo, leave her alone. Delaney didn't come here for you."

Theo held up his hands. "But that doesn't mean we can't spend some time together," he said to Preston. Back to me, he asked, "Are you seeing anyone?"

My eyes flicked to Preston and back to Theo. "No," seemed like the most honest answer because I was in an arrangement, not a relationship.

Preston's eyes lost their amusement, and his jaw clenched again. "Let it go, man."

Theo held up his hands in surrender, and Preston relaxed but only a little bit.

I couldn't tell if he was jealous or if he simply wanted Theo to leave me alone. My new acquaintance was blond with broad shoulders and a classically hand-some face, and I pictured him as the typical frat guy back in college. I was curious as to what kind of lawyer he was. He seemed to like to joke, but I could also see him being very serious when it came to his career and his clients.

I could also see myself maybe saying yes if Preston wasn't around. It wasn't a given, but Theo had a look that said he liked to have fun in the bedroom.

However, I wasn't going to be spending any special time with Theo, and I didn't want there to be any friction between the two men, so I changed the subject. "You two met at Georgetown?"

"Unfortunately," Preston said, but Theo laughed.

"Yeah. And we're on the panel together on Saturday. What are the odds?"

Oh, so he owned his own firm, just like Preston. I might have been right about him and his career if he had been invited to be on that panel.

"What about you two?" he asked me.

"Preston and I went to the University of Minnesota together for our undergrad degrees, where we had some classes together, but we weren't friends. And while Preston went to Georgetown with you, I stayed at U of M."

Preston had wanted to stay in Minnesota for law school, too, but every member of the St. James family had gone to Georgetown. He'd had to make a deal with his parents that he would apply to law school there if they let him go to U of M for prelaw. I hadn't known his family back then, but I was surprised they'd agreed.

"About a year after we both passed the bar, we met up again at this big law firm we both worked at. We were two of probably a hundred faceless associates, but we used to have some fun nights after work."

Theo's eyebrows flew up, and he scanned me up and down.

"I meant, all of the associates. A large group of us. Not just Preston and me." I shook my head with a laugh. "You're terrible."

Lifting a shoulder, he smirked. "So I've been told. I can

let you get better acquainted with the terrible side of me later."

"You don't give up, do you?"

"Nah, I'm just messing with Preston," he said, and I was almost disappointed. "He's clearly having to hold back from beating my ass."

Preston didn't look amused. "I'm fine."

"But you two seem to still be friends, even after the divorce?" Theo asked.

Preston and I exchanged looks.

"Yes," I answered, hoping he thought the same.

Theo rapped his knuckles on the table. "On that note, I think it's time to get a drink."

I perked up at this. "I didn't know there was alcohol."

"Yeah. They're going to do a speech soon—I can sense it—so I want to be back before it starts." He pointed at us. "You two want anything?"

"Are you paying?" Preston asked.

Theo grinned. "Sure. It's an open bar."

"I'll take a white wine, please."

"Beer for me," Preston said.

"Just like at school," Theo said and left.

"He's interesting," I said.

"Yeah, I suppose." Preston shuffled closer to me and put his hand on my hip. "He's a player though, Delaney. He'll break your heart."

"*He'll* break my heart?" *But not you?* The man who already had.

"Yeah."

Preston obviously wasn't picking up on my real meaning, and now wasn't the time to get into our past.

"Don't worry about me. I'm not going to go on a date with him or anything."

"I can tell you think he's attractive."

"So? I came here with you."

He squeezed my side and growled in my ear, "Yeah, you did. I hope you don't forget that."

Theo came back soon with our drinks, and he was right about the organizers giving a speech. When it was finished, Theo flirted with me a little more but moved on to talk to more people while Preston and I did the same. I connected with a couple of attorneys I'd met at previous conferences, and we had fun, catching up.

The night was coming to an end, and I went to find Preston. He was with Theo again, and I was pretty sure he didn't want us to leave together in case his old classmate thought it was strange.

"I came to say good night," I told the two men.

"Good night?" Theo asked. "It's barely nine."

"We have a full day tomorrow, and I want to take notes of others' presentations before Saturday."

Theo tilted his head. "What's Saturday for you?"

"I'm giving a presentation. My first."

Theo whistled.

Preston watched me, a smile on his face. "Delaney is the youngest female judge in Minnesota. She's doing a presentation on her career and the steps she took to get to where she is today."

Theo's mouth dropped open in what felt like genuine surprise. "Damn. And here, I didn't think you could get any hotter."

"And here, I didn't think you could get any more charming," I joked.

Theo grinned at Preston. "You were fucking nuts to let this beautiful woman go."

Preston's eyes narrowed, and I shifted uncomfortably. I didn't want to discuss or even think about why I'd left him. Someday, I would ask him what had changed—when I had enough courage to hear the answer—and then ask him what had recently changed to make him want me again. But this weekend wasn't the time.

Smiling politely, I said, "It was good to meet you, Theo. I will see both of you tomorrow."

I spun on my heel and headed for the exit. A few seconds later, I was stopped with a hand on my elbow, and I was surprised to see Theo instead of Preston.

"Hey, I know I'm not the one you want."

My eyes went wide. "What?"

"I can see you still have feelings for Preston." He said it so casually, as if his announcement wasn't embarrassing.

Was I that obvious in my feelings?

"But since he didn't know a good thing when he had it, I'd love to take you out."

"Are you..." I paused. "Are you serious, or are you doing this to mess with Preston?"

Theo laughed in confusion. "I'm serious. You're a

smart, successful, gorgeous woman. Of course I want to go out with you."

"Oh, well..." I was going to say I wasn't looking for a relationship, but obviously, Theo wasn't either, or he wouldn't want to spend time with someone who lived in a different state.

"No pressure. I don't want to make things hard for you and Preston." He stepped closer. "But if you change your mind and want to stop by and visit, I'm in room 408."

I sucked in a breath. "That's right next to mine," I whispered without thinking.

A grin split across his face.

Had he heard me? I definitely hadn't meant to say it out loud.

Shifting my gaze to look over Theo's shoulder, I spotted Preston where Theo and I had left him. He couldn't hear our conversation, but he could probably guess what Theo had come over to say to me.

But his expression was blank. I didn't have a clue as to what he was thinking.

"I have to go," I said to Theo and fled the room.

SEVENTEEN
PRESTON

When I got up to the room, Delaney was in the bathroom, so I went out to the balcony to wait, leaving the door open to the cool night air. Unlike earlier, I took a seat on the single chair and stared out into the bright lights of Vegas to my left, trying to keep my eyes from looking straight ahead at the empty balcony of the room next door. I was about to shift my chair away when I heard Delaney.

"Preston?"

"Out here."

A second later, she appeared in the doorway. She hesitated before stepping out. Her heels clicked on the concrete as she moved in front of me.

She winced and glanced over her shoulder at the other balcony and back to me. "I think your friend might have heard me say that I was staying next to him."

Wrapping a hand around her upper leg, I leaned

forward and yanked her closer to me. "There's no *might have*. He did. He knows."

Theo had made sure I knew that his room was right next to hers as he grinned like the Cheshire cat.

Putting her hands on my shoulders, she said, "Crap. What does this mean? Do we have to sneak in and out of our room? Or maybe we should try to get a new one?"

I ran my hand up the back side of her thigh and squeezed. "That depends."

"On what?"

"Why do you think we need to sneak around or get a different room?"

Just because I was a straight man didn't mean I wasn't fully aware that Theo was good-looking—I'd certainly seen plenty of women fall for him when we were in law school. He also hadn't held back in letting Delaney know he thought she was beautiful and that he was attracted to her.

"I don't know if you want him to know that you're staying with me."

I frowned. "Why wouldn't I want him to know?"

"I don't know. Because I'm your ex-wife."

I didn't know what that had to do with anything, but it didn't matter. What mattered was, "Do you not want him to know?"

"Me?" She looked surprised I'd even asked.

"Yeah." I skimmed my palm around the inside of her leg and dragged it up, up, up until I reached her hot center. "You." I slid two fingers over her clit, then inside her as a low moan fell from her lips. "Do you not want him to know this cunt is mine?" My words were accentuated with a deep massage to her G-spot.

Her eyes drifted closed, and she threw her head back as she clutched my shoulders, all while moans filled the air.

"Delaney, I need you to answer me."

Another sound could be heard in the near distance. It was a sliding glass door, but it wasn't ours. It was the one next door.

"I don't care if the whole world knows," she said just as I heard Theo step out onto the balcony next door.

We didn't have the light on, but the lights from the Vegas strip and our hotel room would be enough for him to make out Delaney and me in the dark.

"Do you want to fuck Theo?" I asked as I thumbed her clit.

She shook her head. "No."

"He wants to fuck you."

She opened her eyes and looked down at me. "What do you want, Preston?"

I wanted Theo to see how much this woman was mine. And not just for the weekend.

Pausing my hand, I chuckled in a way that was more warning than from humor. "I'm not sure you're ready for the answer to that."

She ran a thumb over my lips. "I am."

I wasn't sure what came over me because I certainly hadn't planned what I was about to do, but everything in me screamed it was what I needed to do.

DELANEY

"Remember, you asked."

Preston withdrew his hand from my body, and I immediately felt his absence, especially when I had no idea what he was going to do next.

"Turn around, Delaney," he said and leaned back in his seat as he sucked my juices from his fingers and stared at something behind me.

When I spun around, I gasped at what—or rather, who —I saw there.

Preston's friend Theo was sitting across from us on his balcony with a drink in his hand. Even though I could see him, it was too dark to read his expression well, but I sensed he had a smirk on his face.

I'd almost forgotten I was in the middle of a conversation with Preston until he grabbed my hips and pulled me back onto his lap.

One large hand caressed the front of my throat. "Lift your dress and spread your legs."

"But I'm not wearing any underwear." It was a nonsensical argument because, even if I were, I would be showing Theo my panties, which were still private.

Preston's grip tightened ever so slightly as he put his mouth to my ear. "I know. He's going to get to watch me play with your cunt, knowing he'll never get to touch it."

I shivered at the word *watch*. In all our voyeurism

fantasies, we'd never actually had someone watch us. And the thrill and arousal that whipped through me was sharp.

He slid his hand lower and pushed one strap of my dress down until my breast was exposed, which he cupped before pinching my nipple. "And then I'm going to fuck you just like this. You're going to ride my cock until we both come, and if he's lucky, I'll let him watch my cum leak out of you."

Grabbing on to his arm, I rotated my hips over his. "It feels so wrong."

"But also so right."

"Yes," I agreed.

Preston nipped my earlobe. "Lift your dress, Laney. Show him what a slut you are. Let him see that pretty pussy of yours."

He'd said similar words to me on our first night together, but then he had meant someone could see me in theory. Tonight, it was very real. It only made me hotter.

Slowly, I dragged my dress up my legs, exposing my thigh-high stockings first and finally my bare hips. I watched as Theo leaned forward in his chair, and I gradually spread my legs.

I made a move to touch myself, but Preston swatted my hand away.

"No. I touch you first in front of him. I want him to know whose cunt this is." While shoving two fingers into me, he pinched and twisted my nipple.

Closing my eyes, I rode his hand.

"Delaney, take my cock out."

It wasn't easy, but I reached behind me and assaulted his pants until I was able to push them away enough to grab his hard length. "So warm," I said, pumping him in my fist.

"Not as hot as you." He took his dick from me and rubbed it against my wet slit. "Are you ready, Laney? Are you ready to show my friend what a slut you are for me?"

My answer was to slam my body down, driving his cock into me.

Preston stretched and filled me so full, and the moan that came out of me was long and loud enough for all our neighbors to hear. Not just the one paying attention across from us.

"Fuck, Laney. You feel so goddamn good." He moved the hand on my breast to free its partner while his other hand went back between my legs to massage my clit.

Rotating my hips, grinding myself on his dick, I said, "So do you, Pres. I'm going to come so fast."

"And why is that? Because of me or because of him?"

"Both," I answered honestly. "But it's only hot that he's watching because I'm fucking you. I wouldn't care otherwise." Reaching back, I grabbed on to his neck. "I only want him to watch because you're inside me."

Preston growled in my ear, "You keep talking like that, I am going to come before you."

"No, you won't. You always get me off first." *Always.*

Preston shifted his hand to use his thumb to push against the top of my clit while his fingers rubbed below it. His cock pistoned in and out of me at just the right speed, sliding over my G-spot with every thrust. He didn't need to worry about me getting off first.

"That's because you deserve it. You deserve every- thing, baby, and so much more."

"*Fuck. Oh God.*" His words were all I needed. "I'm coming," I cried out.

There was no need to announce it. Every single one of my muscles shook with involuntary spasms as the strongest orgasm of my life exploded throughout my whole body. It fully consumed me, to the point that I almost missed Preston shoving his hips up as he came deep inside me.

Collapsing like a rag doll, I felt his cock continue to jerk as he pumped me full of his cum while he wrapped his arms around me and held me close.

"I can't stop," he whispered.

Reaching between us, I cupped his balls, which were tight from his orgasm, and caressed him there. "It's okay. I like it. I like knowing I made you come that hard."

He shuddered, and just like that, his body relaxed. He continued to hold me for a few seconds until his arms loos- ened. With a shift of his hips, he slipped from me, and I put my hand between my legs to feel his seed leak out of me.

Looking in Theo's direction, I scooped up some of Preston's cum on my fingers and sucked it into my mouth.

Preston groaned and picked me up. He didn't glance in his friend's direction once as he carried me inside.

I had a feeling Theo wasn't going to bother asking me out again.

EIGHTEEN
DELANEY

THE NEXT MORNING, I SNUCK OUT OF BED SO AS NOT to wake Preston. I had seen a little coffee shop near the lobby last night, and I wanted to go down and grab a latte before too much of the hotel woke up and I had to get ready for the first presentation of the day.

I grabbed my leggings and sweatshirt that I'd worn on the plane and headed to the bathroom. After getting dressed, I pulled my hair into a quick, messy bun and made sure my face didn't have any weird makeup lines or marks from the pillow. My eyes were still puffy from sleep, but I looked presentable enough to get coffee.

As I went for my phone on the nightstand to make sure I didn't have any messages from my sister about Paxton, I got distracted by my ex-husband's naked body. He was on his back, sprawled out on the mattress with the sheet lying on a single leg and his crotch, and I realized I hadn't seen him completely nude since before our divorce.

Since we'd started sleeping together again, he'd either had some of his clothes on or it had been dark.

And, *wow*... I'd forgotten how sexy the whole package was. All he had to do was open his eyes and smile, and he'd be ready for a photo shoot.

His left hand was resting on his upper abdomen, and his arm was covering up the spot where my name used to be. I hadn't seen the area yet, and I was curious as to what it looked like. I didn't know anyone who'd had a tattoo removed and had only seen pictures on the internet.

Despite telling myself not to do it—because when I saw the empty spot, it was going to hurt—I didn't listen. Rather than going for my phone on the right side of the bed, I switched tactics and went over to the left side to get a better look.

As my heart started to pound, I knew that curiosity was only a small part of why I was doing this. I needed to see it. I needed to know that my name was gone so I would know that whatever was happening between us was nothing more than sex.

Last night had been wild and adventurous, and this morning, I felt closer to Preston than I had in a long time. There was nothing wrong with being close to my ex and sharing a connection. But I needed to remind myself that it wasn't—and was never going to be—like the one we'd had when we were married. And I needed to do it when Preston couldn't see my reaction. I suspected there might be a little bit of mourning, and I'd rather be able to do it without an audience.

Carefully, I slipped my hand under his, pausing to note his naked ring finger as another reminder of how things had changed, and gently moved his arm out and down from his body.

A small gasp fell from my lips, and I froze as I stared in shock.

There, on his ribs, was the last thing I'd expected.

Delaney

My name was still there in dark black ink.

I wasn't an expert, but I knew it took multiple sessions to laser-remove a tattoo. It didn't look like Preston had even gone once. He also hadn't covered it up either.

Still in a state of perturbation, I wandered over to my side of the bed, like I had planned in the first place. But instead of getting my phone and heading downstairs, I sat down on the bed.

I had no idea what to do with this new information. I wasn't even sure if I should keep it to myself or let Preston know I knew.

First, I should maybe try to figure out why it was still there.

My clit suddenly throbbed in my pants, as if to say, *You know why it's still there.* For the same reason my piercing was.

Because we still meant something to each other.

"Delaney."

Slamming a hand over my chest, I jolted a foot off the mattress.

Preston laughed. "Sorry, Laney. I didn't mean to scare you."

I shifted ninety degrees and bent a leg on the bed. "I thought you were still sleeping."

"I was until five seconds ago. What were you doing there, staring off into nowhere?"

I was trying to figure out if he wanted to keep his tattoo a secret or not. Just because he was naked now, it didn't mean he hadn't been trying to hide it, especially since I hadn't seen it so far. And he certainly hadn't pointed it out when he found out I still had my piercing. Although I had immediately fled the room after that revelation.

I didn't know what to think, and I certainly didn't know how to answer him, but thankfully, I didn't have to because he asked another question right away.

"You're not regretting last night, are you?" He took my hand in his. "I hope I didn't push you to do something you didn't want to do. In the moment, it just—"

I squeezed his hand. "I'm not regretting anything." My discovery was starting to really settle in my brain, and I felt even less regret than I'd had when I woke up, if it were even possible. "Seeing your old friend might be a little awkward, but we're all adults. I'm sure after a few minutes of stiff hellos, we'll move on like it happened years ago."

Preston grinned and, in a flash, grabbed my legs and yanked me half under him as he rolled over. "I don't think he'll ever forget the sight of you coming. Trust me. I've seen it a million times, and I'm still awestruck every time."

Heat flushed my cheeks at his compliment. "I was just a woman having an orgasm, Pres. There's nothing special about me. You could get on the internet right now and find hundreds doing the same thing."

"Nah." He pushed my sweatshirt up and kissed my stomach. "That's where you're wrong. You are very special." He frowned. "And why are you wearing clothes? I brought you to bed naked last night."

"I was going to go down and get something from the coffee shop."

"Can I convince you to wait?" he asked as he tugged my pants down bit by bit, kissing my belly as he went.

I smiled. "I don't know if it will take much."

Preston was silent, and I lifted my head to find him staring down at me.

"What's wrong?"

He ran a finger across my bikini line. "Your scar. I almost didn't notice it."

Shoving an arm under my head, I said, "I know, right? It's hard to imagine a whole human being came out of that little area." Whenever I looked at it in the mirror, it didn't seem big enough to me.

Preston kissed my scar and laid his head on top of it.

Using my free hand, I ran my fingers through his hair. "You okay?"

I meant it as a half-joke, but when he looked up at me again, there was pain in his eyes.

"Pres, are you—"

Music blared, filling the room, as my phone rang. I reached over and checked it.

"It's my sister." Sliding the green button over, I answered the phone on speaker. "Hello?"

"You decent?" Natalie asked.

Preston helped me pull my pants back up.

"Yeah. Why wouldn't I be?"

"I thought maybe you'd found a stranger to rail you last night."

My eyes went to Preston, who stifled a laugh. I was glad to see he was in a good mood again. But it was in the back of my mind that I needed to ask him later what had come over him before Natalie called.

I grinned. "Even if I had, I wouldn't tell you."

"What? I'm your sister."

I laughed. "Nat, you did not call me to ask me about my sex life."

She sighed. "You're right. Paxton wants to say hi. Can you do a video call?"

"So, that's the real reason you asked if I was decent."

"Yeah."

"I can do a video call."

Preston rolled off the bed and nonchalantly strolled to his suitcase and took out some clothes. He was so sexy, and as I watched my name move on such a beautiful body, it took my breath away. I was completely mesmerized by the fact that he had done nothing to cover it up. He wasn't trying to hide it from me.

Grinning, he turned around and raised an eyebrow.

I frowned.

Silently, he shook his head and pointed to my phone.

I looked down just as Natalie said, "Delaney? Hello? Are you still there?"

Great. Preston had just caught me gawking at his body like a teenager. When I turned his way again, he was laughing at me.

"I'm here. Sorry about that."

"So, can you talk to Paxton right now, or should I call back later so your mystery man can rail you again?"

Preston threw his head back and covered his mouth so as not to make any noise. Even my sister had figured out over the phone that I had sex brain.

"You're not funny. Put Paxton on the phone, you brat. I want to talk to someone who actually loves me."

NINETEEN
DELANEY

LATER THAT AFTERNOON, I WAS SITTING IN THE BACK of one of the conference rooms, listening to a presentation by a woman who was a veteran in our field, and taking notes.

The air around me changed suddenly, and Preston slipped into the vacant chair next to me.

"How's it going?" he whispered.

"Good."

He put an arm on the back of my chair as he put one leg up over his knee.

It was such a guy move, and I had to smile.

His brow furrowed, but he smiled back with a small head tilt. "What?"

"Nothing." I held up my notepad. "I got some ideas."

While I was pretty much one hundred percent prepared for my own presentation tomorrow, I thought it wouldn't hurt to see how the audience responded to others.

My goal was to be informative, but I didn't want to bore anyone.

Preston and I sat in silence until the current presentation and the Q and A after were finished.

After it was complete and half the room started filing out, Preston said, "I know you're nervous, but you're going to do great. You had my full attention."

This morning, after I'd talked to Paxton and gotten coffee, he had encouraged me to try out my speech with him, and he'd helped me work out a few kinks.

We stood as the crowd started to clear so we, too, could leave.

"Thank you for your vote of confidence. I think doing Women in Law has been good practice for tomorrow, but kids and teenagers are not the same as adults who are our colleagues."

He grabbed my hand and squeezed. "I understand, and if you want to go over it again after dinner, we can." He quickly let go as the group of people thinned, and we followed them out.

After we moved away from the conference room and the other attendees, I turned to Preston. "Thank you, but once was enough. However, I'm thinking maybe I should try to open with a joke," I said even though I wasn't a funny person.

Cupping the back of my neck, he rubbed his thumb under my ear. "Don't force anything. Do what comes natural to you."

"Yeah, like that little show you put on for me last

night," was the first thing Theo said to us after Preston and I had sex in front of him last night.

He was sitting on a padded bench with his phone in his hand, which he shoved into the inside pocket of his suit jacket as he stood.

Preston's hand tightened on my neck, and he brought our bodies closer. "Don't get used to it. It was a one-time thing," he warned his friend.

"Such a shame. You two should start an OnlyFans page."

I looked at Preston.

"Don't even think about it," he said to me while keeping his eyes on Theo.

I really hadn't. Not with my career as a judge. Although I'd probably make more money.

Actually, maybe not. Maybe if I were twenty years younger.

"Yeah, I don't think anyone wants to see my thirty-eight-year-old body. But I bet Preston would make bank," I said with a grin.

His arm moved from my neck to my hip as he frowned at me. "Don't say that."

"Don't say what? That you would make money, getting naked in front of a camera?" I'd only been teasing him even if it was true.

"No. About yourself. You have a beautiful body, Laney."

"Preston's right. You have a banging body, Laney."

Preston's eyes turned fierce, and he swung his head in

Theo's direction. "One, that will be the last time you talk about her body. Two, no one calls her Laney but me. Three, I swear to God, Vanderpool, you so much as touch a hair on her head, and I will make you regret ever getting to see our little show last night."

"Okay, okay." Theo put his hands up and rolled his eyes. "Sheesh. Are you sure you two aren't still married?"

"Our relationship is none of your business."

It was time to talk about something else.

"Let's all just admit, last night was fun, but it was a one-time thing. It won't be happening again," I said.

"I'm a little relieved," Theo admitted.

This made my eyebrows shoot up, surprising me.

"You two went at it all night. Bang, bang, bang—"

"All right, that's enough," Preston said as he swung us around and away from his friend.

"We'll be quiet tonight," I said over my shoulder.

"We will?"

"I have my presentation tomorrow morning. I need to sleep."

"Looks like we're going to bed early because I love seeing you naked and I refuse to keep my hands off you all night." He smiled. "But I will give you a nice orgasm that will put you right to sleep."

"You're such a gentleman," I said dryly.

"I try."

The next morning, Preston woke me up with his tongue between my legs. After he brought me to climax, he slid into me and rocked us both to orgasm—my second of the morning.

After, he lay in my arms while I ran my hands up and down his strong back. He was still inside me, and it seemed he didn't want to leave as much as I didn't want him to go.

I was nervous about my presentation, but we only had one more night left after this. Tomorrow, we were going home after the conference wrapped up.

Not only would he go back to his life and I would go back to mine, but we'd also have to share both of them with a toddler. I loved my son to pieces, but it was nice to spend time with Preston, just the two of us, like it used to be. Before things changed.

"I had an idea."

"Hmm?" he asked from the crook of my neck.

"Let's skip the party tonight." A party in the loosest sense of the word was what the hosts of the conference were putting on tonight. "Let's go do our own thing. It's our last night in Vegas, and you and I will be done with our conference stuff by this afternoon."

I hadn't wanted to do anything last night because I was no longer in my early twenties. I needed sleep if I was going to do a good job today. And the night before, we'd gotten too caught up in each other to go out after we put on the show for Theo.

Preston took a deep breath and rose up on his forearms. "I think that sounds like a lot more fun than hanging out with a bunch of stuffy lawyers."

"You're all hooked up and ready to go." The IT guy pointed to the projection screen behind me to show me that it was a mirror image of what was on my computer.

"Thank you."

"You're welcome. I'll just be in the corner if you run into any problems."

I smiled nervously. "Thanks."

He jumped off the small stage, and I was alone.

People were still coming into the conference room, and I didn't know if it was a good thing or a bad thing. I wanted them to be interested in what I had to say, but also, the more people who came in meant there was that many more to silently judge me.

I knew deep down that I was getting into my own head. The audience wasn't even everyone at the conference, much less every lawyer in the country. I could do this.

Still, it was hard to keep that in mind when it seemed like the whole hotel had arrived and the lights were dimmed on everyone but me.

I was given the signal to start, and I took a deep breath. Grabbing on to the podium, I said, "Good morning. My name is Delaney St. James, and I am a family court judge for Hennepin County in Minnesota."

The doors opened in the back, and a lone figure stepped into the room. Even though it was dark, I knew immediately that it was Preston.

A sense of calm came over me, and I realized I really could do this. He'd been my rock for so many years and through all of my career changes, and it looked like, today, he still was.

TWENTY
PRESTON

"I CAN'T BELIEVE WE HAVE TO GO BACK HOME tomorrow," Delaney said and took a sip from her cocktail.

It was later that night, and all our responsibilities with the conference had been completed. Granted, mine had been easier than Delaney's, but I was still glad to be finished.

And now, we were currently relaxing at a bar. When we'd discussed where to go, we'd opted for a bar rather than a nightclub full of people a decade younger than us. It'd turned out to be a good decision because we'd skipped the tables and booths to sit at the love seat in the back.

"The trip went fast," I told her. Too fast. I liked having Delaney in my bed every night.

"It did. But I do miss our little guy." She threw her head back and sighed. "Parenting. Who knew it would be so hard?" she said when she looked at me again. "There are times when I just want to get away from Paxton, but then, when I do, I miss him so much."

I smiled. "I miss him too."

Earlier that morning, Delaney had told her sister she'd messaged me to come to her room so I could also talk to Paxton. Seeing him and not being able to hug him was hard.

"But since we're here and we can't go home to him until tomorrow, we might as well make the most of tonight."

"I agree."

"But first, I need to use the ladies' room." Delaney stood. "I'll be right back."

"I'll be here."

While I waited, I pulled out my phone. I didn't spend much time on social media because I usually didn't have a lot of time, but since I was waiting for Delaney to come back and I had nothing else to do, I pulled up my app.

I had way too many notifications, and I was scrolling through them to see which ones I wanted to click on when I saw something about my memories from this day to look back on. It started with the most recent year, which was two years ago, and moved backward.

The very last memory hit me in the gut.

It was the day I had proposed to Delaney. I'd forgotten what day I'd actually done it because it wasn't a big spectacle or a special occasion. We'd been living together, and I'd bought the ring several months earlier. I'd actually been trying to find the perfect time to ask her until, one night, we were lying in bed together after making love, and it hit me that I never wanted to be apart from the woman beside me.

I hadn't second-guessed myself. I'd just thrown back the covers, gone to my dresser, pulled out the ring box from the back of my underwear drawer, and asked her right there. Grinning, I remembered how I hadn't even stopped to put on underwear, but Delaney hadn't cared. She'd thrown her arms around me before she finished saying yes.

The picture on my social media page was Delaney's ring in the foreground and the two of us kissing in the background. We were blurry, but you could tell Delaney had the sheet wrapped around her breasts and I was shirtless. My mother had been furious when she saw it, but I'd refused to take it down.

"I'd love to know what you're smiling about," a feminine voice said.

I looked up just in time to see an attractive woman sit beside me. She was with two other women who took the two lounge chairs near each end of the love seat. If I had to guess, they were slightly younger than me, around their mid-thirties.

Putting my phone in my lap, I said, "I was scrolling through my memories and came across the photo of the night I'd proposed."

The woman's smile dimmed for a moment, but she didn't get up to leave right away. Instead, she made a point to look at my left hand. "You're married?"

I considered saying yes, but I didn't want to lie. "Divorced actually."

She looked at her friends and back to me. "In that case, do you mind if the three of us sit here?"

All three ladies were beautiful, and I could tell that at least the woman beside me was interested in me. But the feeling wasn't mutual. However, it seemed rude to tell her that her and her friends couldn't sit by me.

"Sure," I said as I spotted Delaney.

She raised her eyebrows at me as she approached. "I see you've made some friends," she said with a smirk and looked at the love seat.

While there was room enough for three people, it would make it a tight fit, so I took her hand and tugged her onto my lap, where she snuggled into me.

"I just met them. We haven't even made our introductions," I told her and turned to the women. "I'm Preston, and this is Delaney."

The lady who'd sat down next to me gave us both a polite smile and stood. "We didn't mean to interrupt. We'll find somewhere else to sit."

"No, really, we should move. There are three of you and only two of us. We weren't even using the chairs." Delaney moved to get up.

The woman put up her hands. "No. You were here first. It's only fair."

"Well, thank you." Delaney leaned back into me, and I tucked an arm around her.

"We're fine with you sitting here too," I said. I liked having Delaney so close.

"No, thank you," she said. Her friends turned to leave, and she was just about to follow when she hesitated and turned back. "It's none of my business," she said to Delaney, "but you two look very cozy, so you should know he was grinning like a fool over pictures of his ex-wife a few minutes ago." With a nod, she spun around and followed her friends.

I watched her walk away, speechless. "I don't mean to sound like an egotistical dick, but did she do that because she was jealous?"

Delaney, who had also been staring, closed her mouth, and tilted her head. "No. I think she was genuinely warning me. Hmm. I'm impressed."

"Impressed?"

"Yeah. She didn't have to say anything to me, a stranger, but she did."

"She was looking out for you?"

"Yeah. Especially since she was obviously interested in you." Delaney smoothed her hand over my chest. "Not that I blame her. You are a very sexy man. I can't even imagine the number of women you've dated since we split up."

I shrugged. "Only a few. And all of them were set up for me by my mother." She was determined to get me married again.

Delaney stifled a laugh. "Sounds fun."

Taking a sip of my drink, I gave her a deadpan look. "You and I both know it wasn't."

This time, she didn't hold back her chuckle. "Okay, so maybe *dating* wasn't the right word. Tinder was invented after you and I got married. You don't have to go on a date with anyone to sleep with them. How many have you slept with?" Delaney picked up her cocktail.

Well, that was an easy answer. "None."

Her glass was halfway to her lips. "You're not serious."

"Why wouldn't I be?"

"Preston."

"Delaney."

She shook her head, as if she was confused. "Since me, you're saying you haven't had sex with anyone besides...me?"

I nodded. "Yep."

"Not even the night of Vivian's St. Patrick's Day party? You left because you had plans."

"With friends. Not a date."

"Holy shit. I can't believe you haven't been with anyone."

Studying her, I asked, "Why?"

"Because you're sexy, Preston. And I know how much you like sex."

Yeah, with you.

I shrugged. "How many men have you slept with?"

She winced. "Two. But it was only one time each."

I threw my head back and laughed.

"What's so funny?"

"You're judging me for zero sex while you had sex twice."

Her spine straightened. "I wasn't judging you." She relaxed with a sigh. "I was just surprised, is all." She wrinkled her nose. "It wasn't even good."

I liked the sound of that way too much.

"It doesn't bother you?"

"That you slept with someone else besides me or that you had lousy sex?"

She gave me a look because we both knew what she'd been asking.

Lifting a shoulder, I said, "Maybe a little, but since you didn't come, it makes me feel better."

"Who said I didn't come?"

I laughed. "You did by saying the sex wasn't good."

"Oh. Yeah."

"I take it, neither of them went down on you?"

She shook her head. "I didn't want them to."

"Why? Because you didn't want them to see my piercing on your clit or because you really didn't want them to?"

"I really didn't want them to. But they also didn't ask."

Fools. "Their loss. My gain."

I loved her pussy and going down on her. I never understood how anyone couldn't like it.

"They wouldn't have done as good of a job as you anyway."

"Sounds like they didn't do as good of a job as me fucking you either."

"Nobody does."

I growled and rubbed her ass over my hard-on. "You keep talking like that, and I'm going to take you right here."

Delaney grinned at me.

I shook my head with a laugh. "You little minx. You like the sound of that."

A waitress came over, and we ordered another round of drinks and moved on to other conversation.

We stayed for a couple more hours until there were too many people to really relax anymore. Delaney had moved off my lap a while ago, and we decided it was time to let someone else have our spot.

When we got outside, Delaney tripped, and I half-caught her as she ran into me. We both started laughing like only people who'd had too much to drink did.

I blinked a couple of times and tried to shake my head to clear it. "I think we might have overdone it."

"We didn't even have that many," Delaney protested.

"I know. But I can't drink like I did when we were in our twenties."

She fell against my chest on purpose this time. "I know. It makes me feel so old."

Chuckling, I wrapped my arms around her. "You're not old. Because if you're old, I'm old, and I refuse to accept that."

She laughed into my chest before gasping and looking up at me. Slapping her hands over my pecs, she said, "Hey, you never showed me the pictures your crush in there was talking about."

I had to really think about what she was asking me, and I still came up with nothing. "Huh?"

"The lady earlier...after I came back from the restroom. She said you were 'grinning like a fool' over pictures of me. But I forgot to ask to see them."

"Oh." With a quick pat-down, I found my cell in my left pocket and pulled up the image. "It was really only one picture," I said, handing her my phone.

All humor left Delaney's eyes as they filled with tenderness. "Oh my God, the night you proposed."

"It was thirteen years ago today."

She ran her finger over the screen, as if she wished she could touch us. "We were so happy," she whispered.

"Yeah, we were," I whispered back.

She looked up at me. "Preston, why haven't you had sex with anyone since I left?"

I brushed my thumb down her cheek. "Because none of them were you, Delaney."

TWENTY-ONE
DELANEY

"Because none of them were you, Delaney."

His words shoot straight to my heart.

"We've been so happy the last few days. It's almost like the last two years didn't happen." I look down at the picture of our proposal announcement again. It hurts to look at it. "A part of me wishes they hadn't."

But that's what it is. Wishful thinking. Because I'm no longer his wife and he's no longer my husband.

"What if we could do the closest thing to making that happen?"

Forcing myself to look away from Preston's phone, I eye him speculatively. "And how would we manage that?"

"We could get married again."

A small laugh bursts out of me. "What?"

"We're in Vegas, Laney. The capital of spontaneous, last-minute marriages. We could go to a chapel and be together again"—he snaps his fingers—"just like that."

"But what about..."

"What about what? Our families? We already did the big engagement party and wedding. We don't need to do that all again for them."

He has a really good point.

"I can't believe I'm actually considering this."

"I'm glad you are."

"But why? Why do you want to marry me again, Pres?"

He hauls me into his arms and growls, "Because I lied earlier. Mostly to myself. I hate that you had sex with someone else. I want to be the only one who gets to be inside you for the rest of our lives, Laney."

It's not the most romantic proposal, but it's somehow enough for me.

I nod. "Let's do it."

Preston steps back and gets down on one knee. "Delaney St. James, will you do me the honor of being my wife...again?"

"Yes." I tug on his arm. "Now, get up before someone else walks out of the bar and sees you."

Preston stands and grabs my hand, and we head—

Music jolted me from my dream, and I groaned into Preston's chest, which I was pretty sure had my drool on it. Rolling onto my back, I put a hand over my eyes to block out the bright desert sun. My head was killing me, and the ringing from my phone didn't help.

Preston put his hand on my bare thigh. "Laney, please make it stop."

My main focus was finding silence again, so I didn't even think about what I was doing when I picked up my cell. The second I saw it was a video call from my sister, I should have hit Ignore, but since I had killed off a few brain cells from drinking last night, I answered instead.

"Hello," came out raspy and low, and I cleared my throat. But when I saw the face on the other side of the phone, I couldn't help but smile.

"Mommy!" Paxton yelled when he saw my face.

I rolled away from Preston so I could rest my cell on the bed. "Hey, baby."

He looked so cute in his pajamas with his mop of messy hair sticking up all over.

"Mommy misses you so much." At that moment, I wanted to be home with him so badly, and the feeling almost overwhelmed me.

"I miss you too, Mommy. And Daddy. Where's Daddy?"

My sister appeared in the frame. "Honey, your daddy is—"

"Hey, buddy. I'm right here," Preston said, wrapping an arm around my waist.

Natalie gasped.

Oh shit. I was going to hear it now.

"Hi, Daddy! Auntie Natawie says you're coming home today."

"That's right. Mommy and I are both coming home."

"Yay! I can't wait."

"Me neither," Preston said.

"Same, baby. We'll see you soon, okay?" I said.

"Okay, bye." Apparently, Paxton was done with the conversation just like that because he handed the phone to my sister and ran off.

Preston closed his eyes, and there was a possibility he fell back asleep. I couldn't quite tell because I could only see him in the tiny rectangle on my phone.

Natalie shot me a look that said I had a lot of explaining to do. "Really?"

I could practically picture her tapping her foot.

"Not now, Nat. I have a headache."

"*Surrounded by a bunch of lawyers*, you said." Natalie mocked my words back at me.

I sighed. "Can we please talk about this later?"

"Oh, you bet your ass we're talking about this later."

"Delaney is a fucking adult, and she can have sex with whoever she wants."

Apparently, Preston wasn't sleeping.

But I didn't want the two of them to get in a fight, so I cut her off before she could say another word. "I'll see you this evening." I hit End and set my phone down.

Preston was quiet again, and his breathing was deep.

"Pres?"

"Hmm?" It came out more like a grunt.

"What do you remember about last night?"

He rolled away and onto his back, and I turned to face him.

"We went to that bar and had too much to drink." He frowned and then laughed. "You almost biffed it outside."

I remembered that too. "But you caught me."

"More like you fell into my arms."

"I'm a graceful drunk. What can I say?"

He smiled.

"Do you remember anything else? My brain is kind of foggy after that, but I had this dream this morning..." Part of it had felt so real, but yet I couldn't form a complete memory of it. I lifted my left hand, but it was just as bare as it had been the day before. Maybe the alcohol had made my dream more vivid.

"I remember being outside, and then suddenly, we were back here at the hotel." Preston's brow furrowed. "I don't even remember how we got to our room."

At least he had that.

"It's worse for me. I don't even remember coming back to the hotel. All of a sudden, I remember taking my clothes off, but nothing before that."

"So, you remember us having sex?"

"Which time?"

He laughed again. "I'm glad you didn't forget that."

I shook my head, not finding any humor in the situation. "I'm embarrassed that I let myself get so carried away. I'm almost forty. I'm a mother. We were so irresponsible."

Preston cupped my cheek. "Hey. We didn't have that many drinks. They were just really strong. And just because we're almost forty doesn't mean we don't get to have fun anymore. Also, Delaney, you are more than a mother. Please don't beat yourself up."

"You're right."

"If it helps, I'm pretty sure we walked home. It must have cleared some of the alcohol out of us, and that's why we remember being back here."

"It does help."

"Can we go back to sleep now?"

"No."

"What? That was a joke, right?"

I showed him the time on my watch. "We have to get ready for the farewell speech."

Preston groaned and rolled over. "This is bullshit."

"Would it help if I brought you some pain meds?" I was assuming he had a headache, just like me.

"Maybe." He looked at me over his shoulder. "You know what'd make me feel better than that?"

"What's that?"

"You let me fuck you in the shower. I heard orgasms are great pain relievers."

Preston and I managed to make it through the rest of the conference and to the airport in time. This morning had been busy, and with waking up late and our hangovers, I'd failed to enjoy our last morning together.

And now, we were on a plane back home to Minnesota. I knew I couldn't change the past, but I was mad at myself for getting drunk last night and wasting what little time I'd had left with Preston.

I was trying to focus on the good part. Getting to see Paxton again.

Turning my head to watch Preston nap, I gently picked up his hand and held it while he slept.

I just wished I could have both.

If only my dream last night had been real. If only Preston had really proposed again and I got to go home with him. Sure, it would be messy with our family and friends, but we'd figure it out. Especially if we had each other.

When I closed my eyes, a single tear ran down my face, and I hastily wiped it away.

I was getting caught up in wanting things I couldn't have again. I'd played the what-if game so many times after I left Preston. *What if this had happened? What if that had happened?* It only prolonged the pain.

I dropped Preston's hand and faced my window.

If I were smart, I wouldn't put myself through all that again. I needed to stick with my reality because that was where I was living. Preston and I still had our arrangement. And that was going to have to be good enough for now.

Even though, deep down, I knew it wasn't going to work for us forever.

TWENTY-TWO
PRESTON

Delaney had been quiet all afternoon. A sense of melancholy seemed to have descended on her, and I hated to see her sad.

I wanted to tell her to come and stay at my house tonight, but I didn't want to force anything.

"Do you want me to go and pick Paxton up first?" I asked as we drove away from the airport.

"No. Natalie said they just started dinner. I'll let him eat before I go and pick him up."

I nodded in understanding, but I was disappointed. I was looking forward to seeing Pax after being away from him so long.

"Do you..."

Taking my eyes off the road, I raised an eyebrow at Delaney.

She chuckled. "When we get to my house, do you want

to come in for a bit? Maybe we can order takeout, and I can bring Paxton home so you can see him a little before bed."

I smiled. "I'd like that."

She smiled back, and I began planning on how I could stay past our son's bedtime.

Delaney's house wasn't too far from the airport, and since it was Sunday, we made decent time on the drive.

We got her luggage from my truck, and I was a few steps behind her when she suddenly froze just after she reached her front door.

My body went immediately on alert. "What's wrong?"

"My door. I was going to unlock it, but it's not locked." She rubbed the back of her neck. "I swear I locked it before we left on Thursday."

"Stand back."

She looked at me. "What?"

"I know you locked it. I watched you do it." When I reached her, I gestured for her to move away from the door. "Back up, baby. I'm going in first."

The door was already ajar from Delaney, so I pushed it fully open. Thankfully, it was spring, and the sun was still out, so I could see into her place without wondering if someone was hiding in any shadows.

Unfortunately, daylight didn't hide any of the destruction that someone—or someones—had left behind in her house.

We had a clear view into her living room, and it looked like every single one of her electronics was missing. The couch cushions were all on the floor, and her entertainment center was tipped over in the middle of the room.

"*Oh my God*," she said, pushing me out of the way.

I grabbed her arm. "Delaney, you need to call the police."

She pointed her finger toward her house. "I need to go in there and see how much of my stuff was stolen."

Using a calm voice, I said, "Call the police. Then, we'll go in and look together."

She nodded and pulled out her phone. She made the call and was told it would probably be an hour before someone showed up.

After she was finished, I followed her inside.

"They took my espresso machine." She made a disappointed noise. "And my air fryer. Why would they do that?"

"I don't know. I'm guessing they took stuff they knew they could easily sell on the internet."

Her shoulders sagged as we continued on. The dining room that she had turned into a playroom was left alone. Her office was surprisingly tidy too.

"It's a good thing I had my laptop. They took my printer though."

The bathrooms were untouched, and thankfully, they hadn't messed with Paxton's room. Delaney's room was a mess. Jewelry was all over the dresser and floor.

"It looks like they just went for the stuff they thought would be worth money and left everything else," I said.

"Yeah." She moved into her walk-in closet. "What the hell?"

I rushed over to see what had made her upset. Almost all of her clothes were on the floor.

"Why would they do this?"

"I'm guessing they were looking for a safe or hidden valuables." I lifted a shoulder and put my arm around her. "I'm sorry, baby. I don't really know why."

"All my stuff..."

She didn't have to finish her sentence. I had a good guess as to how she felt.

"I don't even have a safe or a place to hide—" She gasped and ran out of the closet.

I followed just in time to see her pull open her bottom nightstand drawer, removing it.

She reached in and sighed. "Oh, thank God," she said, pulling out a ring box. She looked up at me. "My grandmother's ring," she explained, clutching it to her chest.

Nodding in understanding, I suggested, "Why don't you put the drawer back, and we can go wait for the police to show up?"

"Okay." She looked down at herself and must have realized she didn't have anywhere to put the box. "Can you hold it for me until we go back downstairs?"

"Of course," I said, taking the ring box and putting it in my pocket.

She went to put the drawer back and frowned.

"What's missing?"

There was a pile of cords sitting at the bottom, so I guessed she had kept a tablet or an e-reader in there.

"They took my vibrators." She blinked a couple of times. "All of them."

"All of them? How many did you have?" I asked in shock.

"I don't know. A few." She shuddered. "That is so gross. What do you think they're going to do with those?"

I didn't want to think about it, but I hoped they would try to sell them. I didn't want to consider the alternative. "They're probably—"

She held up her hand. "I don't want to know. It creeps me out to even think about it."

She put the drawer back, and I helped her stand.

Pulling her close, I wrapped her in my arms. "I'm so sorry this happened to you."

"Thanks, Pres."

"And I'm sure the insurance company will be happy to reimburse you for all your purchases." I had to chuckle, picturing the insurance agent going through Delaney's itemized list. "But you know, as long as I'm around, you don't need any toys."

"You're pretty sure of yourself."

I raised an eyebrow. "Who makes you come harder? Your vibrators or me?"

"You," she answered reluctantly. "But don't let it go to your head."

"I won't. I already knew the answer. I just wanted you to admit it."

She chuckled. "You're horrible."

"Nah. I was just trying to get you to smile." Kissing her forehead, I squeezed her sides. "If you want to buy a duplicate of every single one of your toys that you lost, I won't judge. And who says you have to use them alone?" Putting a finger under her chin, I lifted her face to mine. "But for the record, I would rather come inside you than anywhere else, every time."

She closed her eyes, and I brushed my lips over hers just as we heard a knock downstairs.

Faintly, we made out, "Police," from the other side of the door.

"Let's go down there and make your report," I said.

Delaney managed to answer all the detectives' questions after she ran through our day and what she'd come home to.

"There have been a few burglaries in the area. I'm guessing the thieves figured out no one was home," one of the detectives said. She was the older of the two and seemed to have more experience under her belt than her partner, who had newbie written all over him.

Delaney sighed. "Yeah. My house was prime pickings for them."

"You couldn't have known, Mrs. St. James," the young newbie said.

"Judge," I corrected from my spot against the wall.

"Huh?" Detective Newbie said.

"She's not Mrs. St. James. You are speaking to Judge St. James."

Normally, I wouldn't point this out, mostly because Delaney didn't care, but I wanted these two police detectives to know whose house they were in. I didn't want them to push her case to the back burner.

Detective Newbie visibly swallowed. "My apologies, Judge St. James. I had no—"

Delaney cut him off, "It's fine. You didn't know."

I stifled a snort. She had informed them of her job when they first arrived. Detective Newbie hadn't been paying attention when his partner was asking her questions, and it seemed like the veteran officer took note.

Looking away, I rolled my eyes. It wasn't any wonder why people didn't trust the police. It was their fucking job to pay attention. Among other things. On the flip side, I'd helped defend cases where cops had paid too much attention to people who were minding their own business and not breaking the law instead of what the city paid them to do.

Veteran Detective cleared her throat. "Judge, do you have anywhere to stay tonight? We'll process the scene, and you should be okay to move back in maybe in a few days, but if you could find other accommodations until then..."

"Oh." It seemed like Delaney hadn't thought of that. "Right. Of course I can't stay here." She ran her hands through her hair. "I mean, yes, I can stay with my—"

"She'll be staying with me."

She swung around, mouth open as she stared at me.

"And you are again?" Detective Newbie asked.

Jesus Christ. Had this kid paid attention to anything?

I pushed away from the wall and stood at my full height. "I'm her ex-husband and friend. And the father of her only child. She can come stay with me while her house is being sorted out. Not only do I have plenty of room, but it will also give our son some stability since he won't be able to stay at one of his homes."

Detective Newbie nodded, reminding me of a bobble-head that people kept on their dashboard. "That's a good plan."

Veteran Detective looked at her partner with disdain before turning back to Delaney. "We have your cell phone and your work line if we need to get ahold of you. We'll let you know when we're finished so you can move back in. We'll get the scene processed as soon as we can."

"Thank you."

"Is Delaney allowed to take any clothes?" I asked.

The two cops looked at each other.

"It's okay," Delaney said before either of them could answer. "I have clothes in my suitcase, and I can wash stuff at Preston's. I should be fine for a few days."

Thankfully, Paxton had clothes at my place, so we didn't have to worry about him.

"Also, we're going to need you to leave your car. Just because it wasn't taken doesn't mean they didn't think about it. There could be fingerprints in or on it."

"Sure," Delaney said without protest. She looked exhausted, and I immediately decided she'd had enough.

"If it's all right with you two, I'm going to take Delaney home now," I said.

Veteran Detective nodded. "It's fine. If we need anything, we'll call."

I took Delaney's luggage back out to my truck and climbed into the driver's seat as she got in on the passenger side. Immediately, she closed her eyes and rested her head back.

Threading my fingers through hers, I said, "Why don't you call your sister and ask her to keep Pax one more night? It's already almost his bedtime anyway."

We'd spent all evening at her house, and it was now dark outside.

"He's safe with your sister, and I can pick him up first thing in the morning."

She lifted her head, nodded, and started to rummage through her purse, which reminded me that I still had her ring box.

I fished it from the pocket of my jeans, and since she was still looking for her phone, I opened it. I was curious as to what she had managed to save from the people who had broken into her home.

Inside, tucked into the slot, was a silver ring with a small diamond. It wasn't big, but that wasn't important. It had sentimental value. There was another ring behind it, which was turned upside down in the little slit as well. At first, I thought it was a plain band, but then I noticed it was two rings soldered together. I pulled it out just as Delaney found her cell.

She did a double take when she saw what I held. "It didn't seem right to get rid of them," she whispered.

I rubbed my forefinger and thumb together, making her wedding and engagement rings sparkle when they caught the light from the streetlights behind us.

I put it back—right side up—closed the lid, and put the box in her hand. "You don't have to explain it to me. I'm just glad whoever broke into your house didn't get them."

Her eyes softened. "Me too."

And because she was feeling so vulnerable, I wanted to make her feel better, so I told her, "When we get home, you can put it in my safe, right next to mine."

TWENTY-THREE
DELANEY

P RESTON TOOK ME TO HIS HOUSE, TUCKED ME INTO HIS bed, wrapped me in his arms, and held me all night. I didn't think I would sleep because my mind was racing, but I fell hard and didn't wake up once during the night.

The next morning, he volunteered to pick Paxton up from my sister's, but I knew I would have to face her sooner or later, so I told him I'd get him myself. I threw on some clothes, borrowed Preston's truck, and headed over there.

I knew I looked like crap, but I'd already called into work, and I didn't feel like doing anything more than I had to. After being at the conference for three days, doing my presentation, traveling, and having my house broken into, I was mentally drained. I just wanted to pick up my son, take him home, and snuggle with him all day. Or at least as much as a two-and-a-half-year-old would let me.

When I got to my sister's, I braced myself for a lecture,

but when I walked inside, Natalie came running and threw her arms around me. "I'm so glad you're okay."

Her surprise reaction had me relaxing in her embrace. "I wasn't home when it happened."

Letting me go, she said, "But you could have been."

"Maybe. The cops said they probably scoped out my place, and when they realized I wasn't home, they broke in."

Natalie shivered. "Ooh, just thinking about it creeps me out." She winced. "I'm sorry."

"No. It creeps me out too." I hated the thought that strangers had come into my home and touched and stolen my things. "I don't know if I'll ever feel safe there again."

"You could always move."

"Yeah."

I'd only owned the house for a year. I'd rented for six months after I left Preston. When our divorce had gone through, I had known I had to decide what I wanted to do for my immediate future, so I'd purchased a house. To turn around and sell it so soon would be a pain in the ass. I probably wouldn't break even with what I owed and what I made on the house. But I honestly didn't know if I could stay there again, so selling might be my only option.

However, I was less than twenty-four hours away from discovering the break-in. I might feel better in a couple of days or even a week.

"We'll see what happens," I told my sister.

"Let me know what you need help with. I'm sure

insurance will want pictures of everything along with the police report. I can help you with all of that."

"Thank you. I guess you're a pretty okay sister."

Natalie stuck her tongue out at me, and I laughed.

She hugged me again, and I asked, "Where's Paxton?"

"Paxton, your mom is here!" she yelled with a grin on her face. In a normal voice, she said, "I was happy to keep him last night, but I could tell he was bummed about not seeing you."

The pounding of little footsteps started from the back of the house and got louder as they moved closer. A few seconds later, my precious baby came around the corner and came barreling straight for me.

He launched himself at me, and I caught him, pulling him into a bear hug.

"Oh, my baby. I missed you sooooo much."

Paxton hugged my neck tight. "I missed you too, Mommy."

I rocked him back and forth for a few seconds, just enjoying the feel of holding him in my arms.

"Are you ready to go, or do we need to pack your stuff?"

"He's good to go. He was packed last night."

"Oh, good. I'm ready to take him home."

Natalie lifted her brow. "You know you are more than welcome to stay here."

"Nah."

My sister opened her mouth, and I could tell she

wanted to say something to me, but she was trying to figure out a way to be diplomatic about it.

"Are you sure that's wise?" was what she came up with.

"No," I answered honestly.

Natalie's eyes widened. She probably hadn't expected me to admit that.

"But it's where I want to be. I know it's probably not smart or wise, but I want to be with him. After I left him, deep down, I thought he was going to come after me, and when he didn't, I felt like I didn't get the closure I needed."

Looking back, I had left rather abruptly because I was trying to make a point. I hadn't gotten to say good-bye to our relationship the way I needed to.

"And maybe that's what I can get from all this because I know it has an expiration date—unlike before, when I thought we were going to be together forever. Maybe my house situation will be exactly what I need to help me move on."

My sister looked like she was about to cry. "Oh, honey, that is so sad." She put a smile on her face. "But I completely understand."

"Thank you." I squeezed Paxton. "Hey, baby, are you ready to go and see Daddy?"

He lifted his head so fast that he almost hit my chin. "Daddy?"

"Yes. We have to go home and see him."

"Let's go then."

I laughed, kissed him, and gave him another hug before setting him down. "Go get your stuff."

As soon as he was out of earshot, Natalie said, "Be careful with Pax."

"I think it will be good for him to stay in one place for a week or so. He just lost one of his homes," I said, repeating what Preston had said last night. "And with Madison still gone, it will be easier for Preston and me to not have to shuttle him back and forth."

"Okay. I get what you're saying. But he might get the wrong idea if he sees the two of you together all the time and you sleeping in his father's bed."

I chewed on my lip. She had a good point. "We will sit him down today and tell him it's temporary. And Preston has a guest room."

Natalie snorted. "That you are going to spend zero nights in."

I shrugged. "Paxton doesn't need to know that."

"Just be careful, okay?"

I nodded. "I will."

Paxton and I grabbed all his things, and I loaded him up in Preston's truck.

"'Tis Daddy's tuck."

"Yeah, buddy, it is."

He held his hands up. "But where Daddy?"

"He's at home. He's working there today so he can see you."

My sister was right. Preston and I were going to have to

figure things out with Paxton, or he was going to be really confused when we moved out.

When we got to Preston's, he came out of his office, and Paxton greeted his dad with the same enthusiasm he had greeted me with earlier.

After Preston set him down, I said, "We need to talk about him." I tilted my head toward Paxton and avoided saying his name.

"Go and play, buddy. Your mom and I have to talk."

"Okay," Paxton said and ran toward the family room.

"What's up?" Preston asked when it was just the two of us.

I rubbed the back of my neck. "I'm worried we're going to confuse Paxton with me staying here."

"How so?"

"He might think we're together if I'm sleeping in your bed every night."

"We are together."

"You know what I mean."

We had an arrangement. We weren't dating.

Preston's mouth pressed into a tight line. "You're staying here."

"I know. I wasn't planning on going anywhere else."

He visibly relaxed.

"But I was thinking maybe I should stay in the guest room."

"No." Preston turned and headed toward the kitchen. "You're in my bed every night."

"I don't mean for real," I said, taking off after him. "Just pretend. Like we can put my luggage and clothes in there."

Opening the fridge, Preston peeked inside. "No. I don't want to lie to him." He grabbed the eggs and went to the stove.

"Won't he be confused when I move back out?"

"So, don't move out."

Preston's back was to me, so he couldn't see my mouth drop.

"Okay, I think we need to have a way bigger conversation than the one we're having now."

He spun around. "Why? I want you here, and you want to be here. Right?"

"Yes, but..."

"But nothing." He kissed me and yelled over my shoulder, "Paxton, Daddy's making eggs. Do you want some?"

I sighed. It was more than nothing. If we were going to have a real relationship, we needed to talk about the past. However, I realized I had only been at his place one night, and I didn't have the mental energy to get into why I'd left him and where our marriage had gone wrong.

If I stayed, we could have that discussion in the future.

TWENTY-FOUR

DELANEY

"I'm here to see Preston."

Two weeks later, I was still staying at Preston's, and we still hadn't had any more conversations about the two of us.

The smart thing for me to do was to move back into my house to create some distance between Preston and me. Being in his bed every night wasn't helping me think straight.

But when I'd gone back to get clothes after the police gave me the okay, I'd packed as much stuff and gotten out of there as fast as I could. I no longer felt safe in my own home. But the truth was, it didn't really feel like my home anyway. I'd only lived there a year. I'd lived in Preston's house way longer than that, and that was the place that really felt like home.

I was digging myself deeper with him, but it was the first time in a long time that I'd felt happy. Like really, truly happy. And even if it couldn't last, I wanted to hold on to that feeling for a little bit longer.

Every time I thought about it too hard, I told myself to worry about it later. I had enough things going on in my life. I didn't want to worry about things until I needed to.

His assistant's eyes darted toward his closed door. "He's taking a phone call right now. As soon as he's finished, I will let him know you're here."

I was meeting with Vivian and Rayne today for Women in Law. Since Vivian had gotten her promotion, she was busier than usual, and she'd asked Rayne and me if we would come to her office instead of going to lunch, like we usually did. I'd immediately agreed so that I could stop by Preston's office first. Paxton had had bad dreams the last two nights and slept in bed with us, and I wanted some alone time with Preston. Funny how I had gone months without sex, and now, after a couple of days, I was sexually frustrated.

I waved her away. "No worries. He's expecting me. I'll let him know."

> Me: Outside your office, but I heard you're on an important phone call. If you let me in, I'll make it worth your while.

> Preston: Come in. Tell her I said it was okay.

"Preston gave me the go-ahead," I told her with a smile.

His assistant stood, but I was already opening his door.

"Sure, we can do that." Preston wrote something down on a yellow legal pad but stopped to look up and smile at me when I entered.

I closed his door behind me, locked it, and marched over to him.

He wheeled his chair back and swung it away from his desk, and I dropped my purse in one of his visitor chairs. When I reached him, I immediately dropped to my knees and went for his fly.

Sucking in a breath, he leaned back to give me better access.

When I pulled him out, he was already hard, and I stopped to admire his cock.

All mine.

Lifting my eyes to his, I found him staring at me. Not his dick, or my hand, or my mouth. But me. My face. And the amount of affection I saw there took my breath away.

He smiled questioningly at me when I didn't move as the person on the other end of his call continued to talk. I jumped up, kicked off my shoes, and shimmied out of my panties as fast as I could.

When I'd found he was on the phone, I had planned to torture him with a blow job until he either hung up or came in my mouth. But after seeing the amount of emotion in his expression, I wanted him inside me. I *needed* that connection with him.

Straddling him, I sank down on his length, burying

him inside me. I flung my head forward as I bit my lip to keep myself from crying out. As always, he felt amazing.

A soft grunt fell from his lips, and his cock swelled inside me as his free hand wrapped my waist and squeezed my side.

I kissed his hot skin. "Do you want me to stop?" I whispered in his ear.

As much as it turned me on to fuck him while he was on the phone, I didn't want to do anything to harm his career or his reputation.

When he tipped his phone away, his only response was, "Don't you dare." Bringing the receiver back, in his normal voice, he said, "Yes, I understand."

He smiled at me until I rolled my hips, and then the look on his face turned to one of pure heat.

I wrapped my arms around him. I buried my face in his neck and rocked my pelvis over his, slowly at first until I found my rhythm.

Preston somehow managed to keep his voice steady, but when he wasn't speaking, his breathing deepened. With every swing of my hips, he urged me on with his arm across my lower back.

Our position was perfect for my piercing, and with every pass it made over his belly, it hit my clit. I continued to move, and just when I thought I was going to run out of steam, my body tensed up, and I exploded. My orgasm tore through me until my legs trembled, and I bit down on his shoulder.

Preston held on to me as I collapsed in his lap, limp and spent from the force of my climax. He rubbed my back as he continued to talk, still hard inside of me.

I closed my eyes and enjoyed the rumble of his chest against my ear. At one point, he rolled his chair closer to his desk on the side where I rested. Lifting one lid, I peeked at him writing something on his pad of paper.

I had to hand it to him; he had amazing stamina because I would have hung up the phone long ago and called back later.

Tossing the pen down, he said, "All right. Mmhmm. Yep. Got it. Talk to you later."

He practically threw the handset in the cradle of the phone and yanked me off him.

"My turn," he growled.

I laughed as he stood and flung me onto his desk with impatience. But my humor soon turned into a moan as he shoved his face between my legs and his tongue in my pussy, encircling my legs in his grip. Dragging his tongue up, he sucked my clit in his mouth until I bucked my hips as I tried to get away.

"*Fuck. Pres*," I groaned, and my legs quivered. "I'm going to come again."

He tore his mouth away and drove his cock into me. "Not without me you're not."

It was a good thing his desk was huge and solid wood because he fucked me with such force that anything else would have slid across the floor or, even worse, broken under the power of his thrusts.

Holding on to the edge, I used my other hand to slip it between my legs and touch myself.

Preston looked down at where our bodies met and back up to me. "The only other person who touches your cunt is you. It's mine, and I don't share."

I nodded. He didn't need to remind me. He was always possessive of me in the bedroom. It was one of the things I loved about him.

"I know."

"I need you to say it."

"I'm yours, Pres."

"That's right. You're my filthy slut. Mine and mine alone."

His eyes flared, pushing me over the edge. I came again, this orgasm shorter but just as sweet. I sensed Preston was right behind me with his own. Sitting up, I forced him back and dropped to the floor. Taking his dick in my mouth, I lifted my gaze up to his as he let go, and his jets of hot cum hit my tongue.

When his climax was done, he helped me up from the floor and kissed me. Gradually, he drew his lips away and sat down, taking me with him. As he tucked me close, I laid my head on his shoulder and melted into him.

Neither of us said anything for a few minutes. I was content with having him hold me. Truth was, I didn't want to leave. I could stay there all afternoon, listening to his heartbeat while he finished his work.

Reluctantly, I checked my watch. "I have to go. I'm already a few minutes late."

I sat up and planted a kiss on Preston's lips before I stood up to put my underwear back on and straighten my clothes.

He fixed his pants and tucked in his shirt, and I slipped on my shoes.

"I'll see you tonight?" I asked even though I already knew the answer. "Clara is making us a new recipe for dinner." I had to admit, it was nice to not worry about what to make every night after work.

Preston shoved himself out of his chair. "I can't wait."

Cupping the back of my neck, he slanted his mouth over mine and kissed me again, slow and deep. By the time he was finished, I was breathless and clutching his shirt.

"I'd better go."

He nodded and let me go.

I looked back at him when I reached the door.

He smiled and gestured for me to leave. "I'll see you tonight."

Forcing myself to leave him, I shook my head at how much I wanted to stay and be close to him. The last time I had felt like this was when I was pregnant with Paxton.

The memory made me smile until I mentally calculated when my last period had been. I stopped walking as a shiver went through me, and all the warmth left my body.

There's no way. Preston had had a vasectomy.

I didn't want to say anything until I knew for sure. All sorts of scenarios ran through my head—from him not thinking it was his to him not believing me. If the situation were reversed, as much as I would want to believe him, I'd have my doubts, knowing I couldn't have any more children. Even though no birth control—even permanent ones —was completely foolproof, we'd only been having sex for a month.

When I did the math, I realized I'd probably gotten pregnant the first night we were together, which would only lead to more doubts.

I had gotten pregnant with Paxton the first month Preston and I started trying, but trying to get pregnant and having an accident were two very different things.

Especially since I knew Preston didn't want any more kids. We'd always talked about having two, but if his vasectomy was any indication, he'd changed his mind at some point.

Telling him was not going to be easy.

I needed to be one hundred percent certain before I said anything to him.

Continuing on, I hurried to Vivian's office before someone stopped and asked me what was wrong and reported it back to Preston. There were probably people who had started at his firm after our divorce, but a lot of them still knew who I was.

Vivian and Rayne looked up when I made it to Vivian's door. Rayne's smile fell, and Vivian's brow furrowed.

Shit. I probably looked as worried as I felt, so I pretended to be out of breath.

"Sorry I'm late," I fake panted.

Vivian smirked and sat back in her seat. "You can give

it up, Delaney. Everybody already knows you were in Mr. St. James's office for the last forty-five minutes."

Rayne started laughing at the same time her jaw dropped. "I didn't know," she pointed out.

Whatever.

At least they thought I was lying because I didn't want to get caught boning the boss rather than because I might be pregnant.

I collapsed into the only available chair and tried to smile at my friends.

But I couldn't fool Rayne.

She leaned over and took my hand, a look of concern on her face. "Do you want to talk about it?"

I felt a burn in the back of my eyes—another bad sign—and I shook my head. "Absolutely not."

Her fingers gave me a squeeze, and she let go.

I had to look away from her before I cried. Not only was I scared about telling Preston I was pregnant—if it was true—but another part of me was also so overwhelmed with hope that I was worried it would swallow me up. I had wanted a sibling for Paxton for so long, and it looked like I might get my wish.

I turned my gaze to Vivian.

She was always levelheaded and not as in tune with emotions as Rayne was, but I had to give her some credit. It seemed she sensed what I needed because she said, "Shall we discuss our next school visit?"

Thank you, I mouthed to her and tried to concentrate on the topic at hand.

But I feared that my time with Preston was about to come to an end, and the worst part was, I hadn't found any closure in my relationship with him. Instead, there was a real possibility I had fallen back in love.

If I had ever really fallen out of it in the first place.

TWENTY-FIVE
DELANEY

THAT NIGHT, IT TOOK FOREVER TO PUT PAXTON to bed.

As soon as I'd left Preston's law firm that afternoon, I'd run to the store and bought a test. I didn't even wait until I got to work. I used the restroom at the pharmacy and found out what I'd suspected was true. Confirmed by two pink lines.

I was pregnant.

After deciding it was best to wait to say something to Preston until we wouldn't be interrupted, I had tried to pretend like everything was normal.

Apparently, I had done a horrible job because as soon as Preston came downstairs after putting Paxton to bed, he leaned against the counter right next to where I was doing dishes and crossed his arms.

"Okay, Delaney, what gives?"

"What?"

He laughed. "Don't *what* me. You've been off in la-la land all night."

I'd been waiting all night to tell him, but now, I was anxious as hell. "Just let me finish the dishes."

Since I'd moved in, we'd been taking turns with cleaning up the kitchen and putting Paxton to bed.

Preston took the pan I was cleaning out of my hand. "Something is obviously on your mind. Talk to me, and then I will help you finish up."

I couldn't put it off forever. "Okay. Let's go and sit down."

I dried my hands and followed him to the table. But after taking a seat, I opened my mouth, and nothing came out.

Preston chuckled as he leaned forward and took my hands. "Laney, it can't be that bad."

It wasn't. Not to me. Despite being nervous about telling him, I was so excited. But I was never going to be able to share that with him if I didn't tell him.

"I'm pregnant," I blurted out.

His smile faltered, and he slowly pulled his hands away. He looked as if he didn't quite understand what I'd told him. "I'm sorry. I thought you just said you were pregnant."

"I did. I am." Leaning back, I put my hands on my lower belly. "I'm pregnant. We're going to have another baby."

Preston stood so fast that his chair fell backward. All

pleasantness disappeared from his face as his eyes narrowed. "No. Absolutely not."

I had known he wasn't going to be happy, but I hadn't thought he'd be furious.

Determined to try and keep the conversation calm, I said, "I think this is something we should decide together. We're both the parents—"

"I said no. Get rid of it."

I flinched, as if his words were a verbal slap.

Taking a deep breath, I stood. "First of all, it's not an *it*. And I'm not getting rid of this baby. I want to have this child."

He stepped forward and got in my face. "Then, you're going to have to do it by yourself."

My jaw dropped. I was completely taken aback that he would say something like that. He loved Paxton so much, yet he was ready and willing to throw his future child away.

"What is wrong with you?" I yelled. "I can't believe you won't even consider us having another child."

Throwing his hands up, he shouted back, "Don't you understand? I can't do it again. I can't go through that again. Do you know how long it took me to move past it the last time?"

I didn't understand what he was talking about. Had he lied about wanting Paxton? Had he faked being happy that whole time? It just didn't seem plausible that he would have been able to pretend for nine months. And I didn't have any doubt as to how much he loved our child. That was completely real. Which left me confused.

"Can't do what? I'm the one who's pregnant. I'm the one who has to go through everything. I'm the one who has to give birth. You don't have to do anything."

Color drained from his face. "Fuck you, Delaney."

I gasped and stared in shock as he picked up his chair and shoved it way too hard into the table. Spinning around, he tore his keys from the key hook and threw the door open before stomping into the garage. He slammed the door behind him, and I stood there, not sure what to do.

It was only after I heard the garage door go up, his truck start and pull out, and the garage door go back down that I realized my little arrangement with Preston had come to an end.

Except, instead of me leaving, this time, he had left me.

The following morning, I woke up in Paxton's bed. I had gone to lie down with him in hopes that I would stay up and hear when Preston got home, but I had fallen asleep and not heard a thing.

It was obviously over between us, with us being on opposite sides of what to do with my pregnancy, but I hoped once he calmed down a little, we could talk about me moving out and what we were going to do with Paxton. His nanny wasn't due to return home for a couple more weeks, so we were still going to have to do pickups and drop-offs ourselves.

I sat on the edge of the bed and rubbed my forehead. Maybe I should have waited to tell him until Madison came back to Minnesota. But I'd had no idea Preston would blow up the way he had. I hadn't thought he was going to be excited, but his absolute refusal to even consider having another baby had shocked me. And his unwillingness to even have a discussion about it was where I drew the line.

Pushing myself off the bed, I went to Preston's room. All my clothes were in there, and I needed to get dressed and ready for work.

When I walked in, I noticed that the shades were still open and the bed was made.

Preston hadn't come home last night.

And just like that, what little hope I'd had for our future—hope I hadn't known I even had until that moment —was gone.

TWENTY-SIX
PRESTON

Delaney: Can you come pick up Paxton
from my sister's after work?

Me: Yes. I'll be there at six.

I KNOWED ON NATALIE'S FRONT DOOR AND WAITED
for Delaney to answer.

It had been two days since she'd broken the news to me
about her pregnancy, and I knew I owed her an explana-
tion for why I had gotten so upset and stormed out. But
when I'd gotten home the next night, she and Paxton were
gone. I'd figured we both needed a couple of days to cool
off before we sat down and talked again.

I heard the lock flip on the other side, but when the

door opened, it wasn't Delaney standing there. It was her sister.

And she looked pissed.

"Hey, Natalie. Is Delaney here?"

She crossed her arms over her chest. "Nope."

"Oh. Do you know where she is? I need to talk to her."

"Why? So you can break her heart again? Oh, wait. You already did that."

I frowned. "Listen, I know I didn't handle her pregnancy announcement well, but in case you forgot, she's the one who left me and asked for a divorce."

Natalie narrowed her eyes at me in disgust. "That is rich. Is that what you've been telling everyone?"

I threw my hands up in disbelief. "It's *true*."

"Because you stopped loving her, Preston. What the hell was she supposed to do?"

All the air left my lungs as I felt physically taken aback by this news. "I didn't stop loving her. When she left, it tore me apart."

Natalie snorted. "Right. You loved her so much that you stopped showing her any affection—she told me it felt like she went from having a husband to a roommate. You loved her so much you did sneaky things behind her back. Oh, wait, I know. You loved her so much that you gave her everything she wanted in the divorce so you could get rid of her. If that's your definition of love, it's no surprise she left."

By the time she was finished, I was grinding my teeth. "You don't understand what you are talking about. I gave her everything in the divorce because I didn't want to drag it out for months and months and put her through all that." My voice had started to rise. While I was trying to remain calm, it pissed me off that she was twisting things around. "And I didn't touch her because I struggled a lot after Paxton's birth. You weren't in that hospital room, Natalie. It was just me. *Me.*"

I was glad Delaney's sister had been spared from everything, but she had no right to judge me.

Natalie studied me, and her face softened. "I knew it was serious but Delaney never said how serious."

"That's because she doesn't know. Not the extent of it anyway. I didn't want to scare her."

"Preston"—Natalie's eyes turned caring—"you need to tell her."

I nodded. "I know."

"Good."

I narrowed my eyes. "But what the hell are you talking about, me sneaking behind her back?"

Some of the anger had left Natalie, but she wasn't ready to give in yet. "She found out about your vasectomy. You'd left your computer on the kitchen table, and your email was open. She had seen the appointment confirmation. Even if you didn't want any more children, you should have told your wife instead of going behind her back to get one."

She looked away and back to me. "You know, she knew you weren't going to be happy about the pregnancy since it had been obvious you didn't want any more kids, but I'm sure the doctor explained to you that it's not one hundred percent effective." She wrinkled her nose. "Did you even go back for the check to make sure there wasn't any sperm left?"

I shook my head back and forth in confusion. "I never got a vasectomy."

"*What?*" She threw her hands up. "For Christ's sake. No wonder she got pregnant."

"I asked her if I had anything to worry about." It was a weak argument, but it spilled out of my mouth anyway.

"She probably thought you were asking about diseases because she thought you couldn't have more kids."

She was probably right, but that wasn't the most important issue I needed to address at the moment. "Does Delaney really think I stopped loving her?"

Natalie's expression softened. "Yes, Preston. You can't go from being unable to keep your hands off your wife to not touching her anymore and expect her not to think something is wrong."

I felt sick. I had failed Delaney. In so many ways. I couldn't stand the thought of her hurting.

I needed her to know how I felt.

"Do you know where she is? I need to talk to her."

Natalie pursed her lips, but a few seconds later, she relaxed and nodded. "I do. She's at the Iron House restaurant."

"Would you mind watching Paxton for a little bit longer? I need to go and see your sister and tell her I love her."

She rolled her eyes. "I suppose I could manage."

I pulled her into a hug. "Thank you," I said and shoved her back so fast that I almost knocked her off her feet. "Sorry. I gotta go."

"Preston," she said as I spun around.

I stopped and looked over my shoulder.

"If Paxton's birth had gone well, would you want the baby Delaney is carrying?"

"It was never about not wanting the baby, Natalie."

"I figured."

"But, yes, I would."

She smiled. "Then, you should know that Delaney already saw her OB, and so far, everything is just fine. But you still need to tell her. Everything."

"Thank you. And I will," I told her and jumped off the front steps and headed for my truck.

As I was putting my vehicle in reverse, my mother's name showed up on my phone.

"Hello?"

"*Preston Charles St. James. Did you forget that I was coming over today? Did you leave your mail out just to taunt me?*"

Fuck. I shouldn't have bothered to answer the phone. Focused on getting to Delaney, I'd answered without thinking.

Because Clara brought my mail in during the week, I had no idea what my mother was talking about. I hadn't touched it for two days since I'd had bigger things to worry about than what junk had been sent to me this week.

I was about two seconds away from hitting the End button, but then my mother said something that had me jerking my arm back.

"Can you repeat that?"

My mother huffed. "I'm sitting at your house, staring at a—"

"Never mind. I'll be there in ten minutes."

TWENTY-SEVEN
DELANEY

"So, has Rayne set you two up with a good lawyer for your new restaurant?" I asked Cade, Rayne's boyfriend, and Beau, her brother.

When Rayne had invited me and Vivian out to dinner, I'd thought it would be good for me to get out and take my mind off things for at least a few hours.

But so far, the only ones to show up were Cade, Beau, and me. Technically, Cade had just finished working for the day, and that was why we were at his current restaurant. But this was only my second time meeting Cade and my first time meeting Beau. Instead of feeling relaxed, I was forcing myself to make conversation so it wouldn't be awkward.

"Not yet," Beau said. "Since she works for the DA's office, I think she said she was going to talk to Vivian and see if she could recommend anyone from her firm."

Lifting my glass of water to my lips, I took a sip,

wishing it were wine. "Good idea. I could also ask—" I was about to say Preston, but I stopped before I offered the two men something I wasn't confident I could deliver on.

"Never mind." I smiled stiffly. "If I think of someone to ask, I will let you know."

Cade's phone buzzed.

"Rayne and Em are almost here. I guess Em picked Rayne up, and that's why they're running late." He looked up at me. "I'm supposed to tell you sorry."

"Rayne is sweet."

Cade went back to his phone and began typing away.

"Oh, you didn't have to tell her that," I said.

Beau leaned over his friend's shoulder and cringed. "*Eh.* That's my sister, dude."

Cade shot him a look. "Don't be reading other people's messages if you don't want to know what they say."

"Well, I did want to know because I thought you were going to tell her what Delaney said. I didn't know you were going to add"—he waved his hand—"all that."

Cade snickered. "Serves you right."

I watched the two volley back and forth and smiled. It was obvious they were old friends, and I was very curious as to what Cade had sent Rayne even if it was none of my business.

Beau looked at me as if he could tell what I was thinking. "He told her, *Delaney says you're sweet. I bet she doesn't know how much of a good girl you really are.*"

My eyes widened as I held up my hand and chuckled.

"It's none of my business. But I'm happy for the two of you."

Beau pushed his chair back. "I'm going to go hit the head before I accidentally see what my sister messages back."

Cade's phone buzzed again.

Beau jumped up. "I'll be back," he muttered and headed toward the restrooms.

Cade leaned back in his chair and grinned. "I only wrote it because he was being nosy."

I put my hand over my mouth to quiet the burst of laughter that came out of me. "I shouldn't laugh, but that's too funny. You two are more like brothers than best friends."

He shrugged. "We've known each other forever. And I hope to make him my brother-in-law someday. Maybe sooner rather than later."

My expression softened. "Congratulations."

Rayne and Cade hadn't been dating long, but since they'd known each other for years, I didn't think they were moving too fast.

He leaned forward and lowered his voice. "Just don't tell anyone. I don't have a ring or anything yet."

I mimicked his posture. "Your secret is safe with me," I whispered.

Someone cleared their throat, and it sounded masculine. I figured Beau had come back and overheard what his friend had to say, but when I looked up, it wasn't Rayne's brother.

"Preston." I blinked up at him in surprise. "What are you doing here? How did you find me?"

"Your sister told me where you were."

"Natalie?" *Since when did she help Preston out?*

"Yes, but she failed to mention who you were with."

I frowned, confused—until I watched Preston look at Cade.

Shit. He thought I was on a date with Cade.

"Oh, no. You don't—"

Preston cut me off with a hand to the back of my neck. "If you don't mind, I need to speak to *my wife*," he said to Cade.

Cade's eyebrows flew up.

"Ex-wife," I corrected. "And I think you said everything you needed to say the other night."

It wasn't entirely true. Preston and I still needed to discuss some things, but he didn't need to come and interrupt my dinner to do it now.

Fisting my hair, he gently tilted my head back. "Wife, Laney."

He released my locks, and when I looked back down, he set a piece of paper in front of me.

Gasping, I snatched up the paper to make sure my eyes weren't playing tricks on me.

CLARK COUNTY, NEVADA
Certified Abstract of Marriage Certificate
Party 1: St. James, Preston, III
Party 2: St. James, Delaney

Date of Marriage...

I put the paper down, having seen enough. "It wasn't a dream?"

The question was mostly rhetorical because the answer was right in front of me.

Preston got down on his haunches and pushed my hair behind my ear.

I had to fight against leaning into his tender touch.

"No, Delaney. It wasn't a dream," he said. "We were just incredibly drunk."

Cade leaned over and looked at what Preston had come to the restaurant to show me just as Beau returned to the table.

Being best friends, they had a silent conversation with a few nods and eye movements.

So, two men I barely knew were about to witness my humiliation.

Tears threatened to spill, and I hated it because I knew it was my hormones. I didn't want anyone, especially Preston, to think I was weak.

I straightened my spine. "Did you come here to ask me for a divorce? Because you could have waited until we were alone."

His brows furrowed in a scowl. "What the fuck? No. I said I needed to talk to—" He groaned in frustration and stood. Snatching my hand, he pulled me up. "Does anyone know where we can go to talk privately?"

"Uh...you can use my office," Cade offered.

Preston nodded. "Perfect."

No, it wasn't perfect, but it was better than being in front of a room full of strangers.

Cade jumped out of his chair. "It's this way."

Preston tugged on my arm, leading me away.

We were walking in the direction of the front when Rayne and a woman I had never seen before, presumably her sister-in-law, came into the restaurant.

Cade stopped to talk with them, causing Preston and me to wait as well.

Rayne slipped her arm around Cade's waist, and he kissed her on the forehead and said something to her in a low voice.

But I didn't have to guess what he had said because Rayne jerked around, and her mouth dropped open when she saw Preston holding my hand.

She'd only met my ex-husband—*husband*—twice, but he was a hard man to forget. I gazed at him from the corner of my eye. At least, he was in my opinion. I couldn't believe he was mine again, only to be taken away so soon.

"What's going on?"

It was Vivian. She and Dominick had walked in now too.

"Delaney and Preston got married in Vegas," Rayne said.

"We're becoming a spectacle," I said under my breath.

"You're right," Preston agreed. "Let's go home."

I wished he wouldn't call it that.

"Pres, can we just—"

He swung me toward him until we faced each other. "Either we talk here or we talk at home."

My friends watched me, waiting to see what I was going to do next.

"Fine. We'll go to your house."

Turning to Vivian and Rayne, I said, "I'll talk to you later?"

"You'd better," Vivian said.

"I need my purse," I told Preston.

"I'll grab it," Rayne offered.

Cade put a hand on her arm. "No, I'll get it. I know where we're sitting."

"Thanks, honey." Rayne's face was so full of love for Cade that I had to look away.

Thankfully, he was fast and brought my purse back in less than a minute. He cleared his throat. "I thought you might also want this." He held out the marriage certificate.

Preston plucked it out of Cade's hand, folded it up, and looked at me. "Let's go."

TWENTY-EIGHT

DELANEY

I FOLLOWED BEHIND PRESTON AS WE DROVE TO HIS house, and when I pulled up behind him, I noticed the fancy car in the driveway. It was the same one that had been there the night he brought me home from our separate dates. At the time, I hadn't known it belonged to his mother because she got a new car about once a year.

When I got out of my vehicle, I slammed the door in frustration. After everything, I had to deal with my ex-mother-in-law. *Actually, I guess she is my mother-in-law again.*

Preston stepped out of his truck and caught me eyeing his mother's car.

"I forgot she was coming over tonight. She's already going to be pissed because I stopped home for two minutes to grab the marriage certificate and left her to wait. But I'm going to tell her we'll reschedule."

I rubbed my forehead and sighed. "Preston, we don't

have to do this tonight. I know we need to talk. We need to talk about what happened in Vegas and"—I had to look away from him—"the baby. If you don't want to have anything to do—" My voice broke, and I had to stop before I finished my statement because the thought of Preston denying his own child hurt like a knife to my heart.

I couldn't imagine Paxton going for visitations while his brother or sister stayed with me. I had no idea how I was ever going to explain that to our future child if it was what Preston decided on. I didn't really think Preston would be so cruel, but he'd been so upset when I told him that I didn't know what to think anymore.

Taking a deep breath to give myself a moment, I continued, "Anyway, like I said, we can talk it through maybe when everything isn't so fresh. Right now, I need to sell my house and find a new place to live. Our new marriage and my pregnancy can wait. We have time."

Preston's footsteps sounded on the pavement, and when I let myself glance at him again, the expression on his face left me awestruck. He looked devastated.

When he reached me, he cupped my face and lowered his forehead to mine. "I guess we're going to do this out here." He lifted his head, his eyes full of conviction. "I made the mistake of letting you go last time because I thought it was the right thing to do. But I've been given the gift of being your husband again, and if you think I'm going to walk away, you are dead wrong. And you don't need to find a new place to live because you're moving back home. Here. With me. I am not losing you a second time." All of a sudden, he went from looking determined to looking scared. "At least, I hope I don't."

Covering one of his hands with mine, I put the other on his chest, where his heart beat frantically. "What do you mean? What are you talking about?"

"Your sister said I need to be real with you, and I know she's right, but this is hard."

"It's okay. Take your time."

"You know how serious Paxton's birth was."

"Mostly."

I had been in my thirty-seventh week, and the elevator had been out at work. Normally, I didn't mind the extra exercise, but at almost full-term, I was miserable. Not only could I barely breathe, but I couldn't see my feet any longer, and as I was going up, I tripped and landed right on my pregnant belly.

At first, I thought I was okay, but when I went to the bathroom, there was a little bit of blood. I decided to leave work early, and I called Preston to meet me at the hospital.

When I got up to labor and delivery, I stood to get out of the wheelchair to move to the bed, and I felt a gush. I thought my water broke, but I realized something wasn't right when the nurses helped me take my black pants off. That was when I saw the blood. I wasn't too scared because they'd hooked me up to a monitor, and I could hear Paxton's heart beating nice and strong. I was only two centimeters dilated, so they told me it would be a while, but that everything was okay at the moment. They gave me some medicine for the pain, and I fell asleep.

The next thing I remembered was waking up in recovery after having a C-section. I was told that the bleeding I'd had earlier got worse and was caused by a placental abruption. They had ended up taking me to surgery and delivering Paxton before things became critical.

"Yes. But I mostly know what happened based on what I was told. I don't remember going to surgery or anything. I just know that everything turned out okay."

"Barely, Delaney. It *barely* turned out okay."

"What do you mean?"

"I know you think you fell asleep, but you passed out. I thought maybe the medication had made you sleepy, but when I tried to wake you, you barely woke up, and nothing you said made sense. I got worried, so I pulled the covers off you in hopes the cool air would get you to respond."

He let go of my face and turned away.

"There was blood everywhere, Delaney. And not just blood, but huge clots. You were covered in blood. Of course, I knew it wasn't good, but when the nurse came in and immediately yelled for the doctor, I knew it was serious. They did a sternal rub on you, and you wouldn't wake up. All the while, more blood kept coming and coming. I was yelling at them to do something, but it wasn't until Paxton's heart rate started to decline that they took you to surgery." He looked over at me. "Did you know they had to give you a blood transfusion?"

"Yes, but I thought that was because of the surgery."

"No. It was because you'd almost died. I thought I'd

lost you...and it fucked me up for a long time." Slowly, he pivoted toward me again. "I know you think I stopped loving you, but nothing could be further from the truth. I was just so scared to touch you again. For a while, every time I did, I pictured you on that hospital bed, where everything that was supposed to be white was red. And forget about having sex with you. The thought of you getting pregnant scared the fucking shit out of me. I couldn't do that to you again."

Covering my mouth with my hands, I fell back against my car. So many things made sense now. Especially the other night.

I'd kept wondering what he had been talking about. *"I can't do it again. I can't go through that again."*

He hadn't been talking about having another baby. He had meant me almost dying.

"But you didn't stop me from leaving. You didn't come after me. You lost me anyway, Preston."

"I know. Because I thought even if I couldn't have you, at least you would be *alive*. I wouldn't get you pregnant again and kill you."

I closed my eyes. It was such a morbid way to think, but it was at that moment when I realized Preston had gone through something incredibly traumatic. Maybe even more than I had. I didn't have any horrible memories of Paxton's birth.

Throwing my arms around him, I hugged him close. "I'm sorry you had to go through that."

Setting his hands on my hips, he drew away, a frown

on his face. "Me? You're the one who almost didn't make it."

I rubbed the spot over his heart. "Pres, that doesn't make your trauma any less real or important."

Gradually, he nodded in understanding. "I guess."

"Is that why you didn't fight me on anything with the divorce?"

"At that point, I was almost numb, and I figured you'd been through enough. I just wanted you to be happy."

I clutched his shirt. "You big dolt. *You* are what makes me happy."

A small smile tugged on the corner of his mouth.

I bit my lip, almost afraid to ask my next question. "So, if we excluded me giving birth, do you still hate the fact that we're having another baby? Did you get a vasectomy because you didn't want more children? Or because you were worried about me?"

He chuckled nervously. "So, I *considered* getting a vasectomy because I was worried about you. I made a consultation appointment to discuss my options, but I never went through with that first appointment, much less had the procedure. And I would have told you before I went through with it. I wasn't sure about anything, so I didn't bring it up to you."

My jaw dropped. "So, we've been having nothing but unprotected sex for weeks?" That explained a lot. "No wonder I'm pregnant."

"That's what your sister said," he said dryly.

"If I had known, I wouldn't have drunk so much."

"Oh shit. You were pregnant then?"

"Barely. My doctor told me it happens to women all the time and I shouldn't worry since it was a one-time thing. But then again, I wasn't able to tell her I got so drunk that I married my ex-husband."

"I'm really glad you did."

He ran his thumb down my cheek, and a memory of that night flashed in my brain, causing me to gasp.

"What?"

I blinked up at him in wonder. "You haven't had sex with anyone but me."

He smiled. "I told you, Delaney, none of them were you. You're the only one I want."

"What changed?" I asked.

"What do you mean? It's always been you."

"How did you go from not touching me to railing me every night for the last four weeks?"

"Four weeks? I can't believe *I* didn't realize you were pregnant."

I tugged on his shirt. "Answer the question."

He snorted. "A shit ton of therapy."

"*What?* Really?"

Preston had never been against therapy. At least, not for other people. But he'd grown up in an environment that didn't approve of mental health care. I'd heard his mother make comments many times throughout the years.

"Yeah. It took months, but I eventually figured out I couldn't do it on my own. But I'm probably going to have to start going back now that you're pregnant." He looked down even though our bodies touched. "I can't believe we're going to have another baby."

"I know. But my doctor also told me not to worry too much about another placental abruption because it probably won't happen again. It was because of outside circumstances. If I hadn't fallen on the stairs, it wouldn't have happened."

"That makes me feel a little better, but I'm probably still going to worry constantly."

That didn't bother me. It meant he cared.

"I understand."

"At least, I think I will worry. I still have to wrap my head around it. Right now, it doesn't seem real."

"Tell me about it. When I found out, I was in shock, especially since I thought you were fixed." I smiled. "I'm glad you're not though. You're the only man I've ever wanted to father my children."

He growled, "You keep talking like that, and I'll knock you up as soon as this one's born."

I laughed but only for a moment. "Are you sure you want to do this?"

"Do what?"

"Be married to me again?"

Preston reached into his pocket and pulled out our wedding rings. "More than anything else in the whole world."

TWENTY-NINE
PRESTON

STEPPING BACK, I LIFTED DELANEY'S HAND AND slipped her wedding ring on her finger. After admiring it for a moment, I said, "Perfect."

Her eyes were filled with awe. "When did you have time to get these?"

I slid mine on, too, and the familiar feel of it was comforting. I'd missed it. "When I picked up the marriage certificate."

She smirked. "So, you were pretty sure of yourself then?"

"More like hopeful." Threading her fingers in mine, I squeezed. "Come on. Let's go inside. I need to talk to my mom."

"Uh...I can wait out here," she offered. Or rather pleaded.

"No. I think it's best you come with me."

What I had to say to my mother was something I

wanted Delaney to hear. I wanted her to know how things were going to be around our house when it came to Rebecca St. James.

We walked through the garage and into the kitchen, which was empty, so we continued out to the entryway.

The lights were on in my office, and I called out, "Mom?"

I heard some shuffling and then, "Preston, it's about time you got back. You raced in here and then left right away before I could talk to you about your mistake."

"FYI, my mother was the one who opened my mail from Nevada. She called me on my way to the restaurant."

"Oh, great. She sounds thrilled," Delaney said dryly.

She was trying to act like she didn't care what my mother thought, but I knew she did. My mother's treatment of Delaney hadn't been responsible for our divorce, but she sure hadn't done anything to help our marriage. I'd often let things go because I didn't want to create scenes, but that stopped today. Delaney deserved the whole world, including a mother-in-law who respected her.

I cleared my throat. "Mother, can you come out here, please?"

"I'm coming. Give me a minute," she snapped.

"How you came out of her I will never understand," Delaney said.

"Honestly, me neither," I admitted.

A few seconds later, her heels clicked on the floor. "I had to turn off your computer. I was researching annul—" She halted when she saw Delaney standing next to me, and she pursed her lips. She straightened her back and stuck up her nose. "I was researching annulments. We can't have you two getting another divorce." Her hand went to her throat. "Can you imagine?"

The woman was completely ignoring our clasped hands, and I had to wonder if my mother was in full denial or if she was just a bitch.

"That's not necessary," I told her. "Delaney and I aren't getting divorced."

"Preston, you're not thinking things through," she whispered, as if Delaney couldn't hear everything she said. "She *left* you, son. She could do it again."

"She left because I wasn't being a good husband, like I'd promised her I would be on our wedding day. I'm just honored she is willing to give me another chance to prove myself."

"And I'm not going anywhere, Rebecca. I love your son with all my heart. We've both made some mistakes in the past, but we are working on rectifying them."

My chest swelled at hearing Delaney say she loved me. I let her hand go so I could wrap my arm around her waist and pull her close.

"Speaking of mistakes, one of them is how I let you treat my wife in the past, and I want you to know that it ends today. You seem to think the last time I kicked you out of our house was a fluke. Or maybe you're just doing what you always do and ignoring things that you don't like, but I was very serious that night. Delaney is an amazing woman, and a wonderful wife, and an excellent mother. I know you think she doesn't deserve me, but honestly, I feel like I don't deserve her."

Delaney looked up at me with love in her eyes.

I love you, I mouthed.

Turning back to my mother, I continued my speech. "From now on, I am going to treat her like the goddess she is. You can treat her with the respect she deserves, or you will be asked to leave. You won't get any warnings. This is your warning. I will not tolerate you disrespecting her. And believe me when I say, you get three chances, and then I will ask you to stay away from us forever."

My mother's jaw dropped.

"Also, don't think you can treat her one way around me and another way behind my back because Delaney will tell me if you are rude to her. And I will believe her. Do you understand?"

"Well, I—"

"Do. You. Understand?" I repeated. "Just remember, if we kick you out of our lives, you won't see either of your grandchildren."

My mother visibly swallowed, and she finally started to look worried. "Grandchildren?"

"Yes. Delaney is pregnant. No, that is not why we got married. We just found out a couple of days ago." I didn't need her assuming anything. But I wanted her to realize the stakes.

"I—I will try to be nicer." My mother looked like she was physically in pain.

But it wasn't good enough.

"Nope." I started walking toward the door.

"Okay, okay. I will be nice." She looked at Delaney and tried to smile.

It was awful and awkward, but at least I felt like she might really make an effort to be nicer to her daughter-in-law.

I smiled. "Thank you. But unfortunately, it's time for you to go anyway."

"But I haven't even seen Paxton."

"He's not here at the moment, and I'm not going to pick him up for a little while yet. First, I need to take my wife upstairs and make love to her."

Out of the corner of my vision, I saw Delaney's eyes widened, and she clamped her lips together as she tried not to laugh.

"But you're welcome to wait if you really want to," I told my mother. I shifted my gaze to Delaney and let her know how much I wanted her. "I don't know how long we'll be though," I said, keeping my eyes on Delaney but talking to my mother.

"Preston, I will be more respectful of your marriage, but there is no reason to be vulgar."

I looked back at my mom and laughed. "That's not vulgar. If I was trying to be vulgar, I would have said, *I need to take my wife upstairs and fuck her until she can't walk the rest of the night.*" I ignored her horrified gasp. "But I didn't. Now, if you will kindly leave. We can set up another time for you to see Paxton."

Delaney's skin was flushed, and her eyes were filled with heat.

"Actually...you know what? You know where the front door is. You can see yourself out." I marched over to Delaney and grabbed her hand on my way upstairs. "Come on, baby. With you looking at me like that, I can't wait any longer."

We were halfway up when she paused to turn around. "Thanks for coming over, Rebecca. We'll have to do this again soon."

We hurried the rest of the way up before I burst out laughing. "You are horrible to taunt her like that."

Delaney tried to look horrified, but she was also laughing. "Me? I'm not the one who said I was going to fuck me."

I lifted a shoulder. "I know. I was trying to remain civil, but she gets under my skin too. And I think the five-year-old in me likes to push her buttons sometimes, especially since I couldn't when I was little."

"It was pretty funny."

Pulling her into our bedroom, I yanked her close to me. "I love you, Delaney St. James."

"I love you too, Preston St. James III."

Lowering my head, I slanted my mouth over hers. I slipped my tongue in her mouth as I undressed her. When we were both naked, I walked her back until she hit the mattress and sat down.

I was ready to push her back and climb over her, but she stopped me.

Gently, she ran her hand over her name on my rib cage before kissing me there too. "I love that you never removed this or covered it up. I know it wouldn't have been as easy to get rid of as my piercing would have been, but it doesn't make it any less special."

I placed my hand over hers on my side. "It wouldn't have mattered if I had gotten it removed. You're still tattooed on my heart."

EPILOGUE ONE
PRESTON

DELANEY SET PAXTON ON THE FRONT STEPS OF HER parents' home and rang the doorbell.

She glanced over at me and chuckled. "You look a little green."

"Of course I do. Your parents already hate me, and that was before all the recent stuff happened."

Taking my hand, she squeezed it. "My parents never hated you. They were almost as concerned about you as they were about me when I told them about the divorce."

"So, the opposite of your sister?"

She laughed. "Yes."

"Daddy okay?" Paxton asked.

"Yeah, buddy, Daddy will be fine," I reassured him. "As soon as we get this over with," I added under my breath.

The lock clicked, and the front door was pulled open as Delaney's mom said, "Delaney, you never ring the bell.

Why didn't you just come—" Evelyn looked taken aback when she saw me standing next to her daughter.

"Nana!" Paxton shouted with excitement and ran into the house to hug his grandmother.

"Hey, Mom. I thought since I brought someone with me, I wouldn't barge in like I normally do."

I had actually asked Delaney not to walk in like she usually did because I didn't want to enter her parents' house, uninvited.

Her mother stood back and waved us through. "Come in, come in." Once the door was shut, she looked up at me. "And to what do I owe the pleasure of seeing you, Preston?" she asked as Paxton ran out of the room.

I glanced at Delaney, who gave me an *I told you* look.

"Henry, come here and see who came to visit us," Evelyn called out to her husband.

A few seconds later, Delaney's father walked in with Paxton in his arms. He grinned when he saw me. "Preston." He held out his hand. "It's been a while."

I shook it and said, "It has, sir."

Henry laughed. "Sir? Since when did you start calling me sir?"

Since your daughter and I divorced.

After learning some things from Natalie, I honestly had no idea how her parents felt about me. I was worried I had lost their respect. Except, unlike my mother, I probably deserved it for the way I had neglected my marriage with Delaney.

"Uh...today, I guess," I answered.

"Well, stop. It's Henry to you."

"And don't you dare even think about calling me ma'am, young man," Evelyn said to me.

I smiled. "You got it."

Delaney clasped her hands together. "Preston and I came to talk to you about something. But I think we should sit down."

Her parents exchanged looks.

"Let's go sit in the living room," Evelyn said.

Delaney, Paxton, and I followed behind them. Delaney and I sat on the couch while her parents sat on their matching recliners. Paxton went directly to the corner of the room and started pulling out toys from the toy box there.

"What do you have to talk to us about, honey?" Delaney's mom asked, a look of concern descending on her face.

"As you know, Paxton's nanny has been out of town, helping her mom recover from surgery," Delaney said.

"Yes, that's right. How is everything?"

"Good. Madison's mom is doing really well, and Madison is planning to come back to Minnesota in a week or so."

Evelyn smiled. "That's so nice to hear."

"Anyway, since Madison has been gone, Preston and I didn't have her to take Paxton back and forth, so we've been seeing more of each other. The first night I took Paxton to Preston's house, he invited me to stay for dinner.

I stayed until Paxton's bedtime, and the two of us had...a nice conversation after putting him to bed."

Usually, I wasn't one to get embarrassed easily, but the mere thought of her parents knowing the dirty things I had done to their daughter on my kitchen table had my face heating.

Delaney seemed oblivious to my shame and continued telling her story. "We also found out that we were attending the same law conference in Las Vegas the following weekend. We spent time together all weekend and had fun while we were there."

Fun wasn't the word I would use to describe being inside her every chance I had gotten, but I understood Delaney couldn't tell her parents all the naughty things we had done together.

I cleared my throat. "Delaney also did an excellent job on her presentation there. You should be incredibly proud of her."

She smiled almost bashfully as her father said, "We always have been."

"Yes, well, besides my presentation, Preston and I—I can't believe I'm about to admit this because it's so cliché—got married again."

Evelyn's and Henry's mouths fell open.

And since we had already shocked them, I took Delaney's hand in mine and said, "And we just found out we're going to have another baby."

Evelyn covered her mouth with her hand as her eyes

filled with tears. "Oh my God, we've been waiting for this for so long."

It was my and Delaney's turn for our jaws to drop.

Henry picked up his wife's hand. "What your mother means is that we know how much you two loved each other, so your divorce never made sense to us. We both understand it's none of our business, and there are things we don't know, but I also know that Delaney never talked about any of her boyfriends the way she talked about you, Preston. And, Preston, I could always see the love you had for our daughter in your eyes. You two splitting up seemed to come out of nowhere. Again, there's a lot we don't know, but we both just never sensed either of you fell out of love with one another."

Wrapping my arm around Delaney, I pulled her close. "Your parents are pretty smart," I whispered to her.

She put her hand on my leg and squeezed. "So, does that mean you're happy for us?" she teased her parents.

Her mother jumped out of her chair as she said, "Of course we are." She opened her arms. "Now, give me a hug." When it was my turn, she said, "Welcome back to the family, Preston."

"Thank you. You don't know how much that means to me."

She patted me on the cheek. "I do. You're like the son I never had." She chuckled and made an oops face. "You and Natalie's husband both," she corrected.

Henry also gave Delaney and me a hug, and then he

turned around. "Paxton, how would you feel if you had a brother or sister?"

"No," Paxton said without looking up from his toys.

All the adults in the room started laughing.

"Son, do you want to see what I've been working on since you've been gone?" Henry liked to work with his hands in his free time, and he was talented at building furniture for fun.

"I'd love to."

As I followed him out of the living room, I heard Evelyn tell Delaney, "You know, I already suspected something was going on when you and your sister said you were staying 'with a friend' after your house was broken into. I hoped it was Preston, but I didn't want to say anything in case it wasn't."

I grinned all the way to the garage.

Later that night, after having dinner with the family—including Delaney's sister, brother-in-law, and niece and nephew—we came home and decided to make it a movie night.

Paxton was worn out after playing with his cousins and was snuggled up on the couch with Delaney. I told them to start the Disney movie while I made popcorn for us. I was only gone for about ten minutes but found them both sleeping when I returned to the family room.

Delaney's eyes popped open, as if she sensed me, and she held out the arm that Paxton wasn't lying on.

Laughing, I handed her the bowl while I sat on the other side of Paxton. "How'd you know I was back?"

"I just know when you're in the room." She grinned at me. "Or maybe it was just my nose that smelled the popcorn."

I put my arm on the back of the couch. "I'd like to think it's me, but I'm not ruling out the popcorn." Shifting in my seat, I reached for some of the fluffy movie snack. I glanced down at Paxton. "Should we wake him? He's going to be up so early tomorrow."

As if he sensed me talking about him, Paxton dragged his head up. "I up, Daddy."

"Okay, buddy. Daddy made popcorn. Do you want some?"

"Yeah," he said and fell back asleep.

Delaney shrugged. "More for us. But you're right about tomorrow morning."

"I'll get up early with him so you can sleep in."

"I think it's my turn."

"Nah. You're busy creating new life. The least I can do is take care of the one we already made."

She smiled dreamily at me. "You're the best."

I snorted. "We both know that's not true, but I love you for it anyway."

Her face grew serious. "We're not going to give up on each other this time, right?"

She'd asked me this a couple of times already, but if I

233

had to tell her yes every day for the rest of our lives, it would be worth it just to be with her.

I leaned over and kissed her forehead. "You bet your ass I'm not giving up. You try and divorce me again, and I'll take you for every penny you have," I teased.

She chuckled. "You wouldn't, but I love the sentiment."

"Only lawyers would think that's a sign of love." I laughed.

"That's why we're perfect for each other."

"You're right; we are."

"I love you too, Pres."

"I love you too, Laney."

EPILOGUE TWO
DELANEY

TEN MONTHS LATER

Ding-dong.

With a grin on my face, I yanked the door open to welcome the visitors. "Hey, guys. Come in."

Rayne, Vivian, Dominick, and Cade stepped inside.

Rayne pulled me into her arms. "Congratulations, Delaney."

"Aw, thank you."

Vivian smiled. "Yeah, Delaney, congrats." She rubbed her hands together. "Where is she?"

Holding up a finger, I yelled, "Preston, they're here."

A few seconds later, he came downstairs with our daughter in his arms and Paxton trailing behind him.

"Mommy, the baby had a poopy diaper. It was stinky. Daddy said a bad word."

"You would have, too, if you had to change it," Preston said, defending himself while I tried not to laugh.

I wasn't the only one. Someone behind me coughed to cover their laugh.

"Hey," Preston said when he reached us.

"Congrats, man," Dominick said.

I took the baby from Preston as he said, "Thanks," with a big smile while he picked up Paxton.

Shifting my arms so everyone could see better, I said, "This is Everly Marie St. James."

"Oh, she's beautiful," Rayne said as I gave her the baby to hold.

"She really is," Vivian agreed.

"I Paxton."

Cade put his fist out. "Put 'er there, Paxton?"

Our son grinned and gave Cade a fist bump.

"You know, I'm a big brother too," Dominick told Paxton, also giving him a fist bump.

Preston put his free arm around me. "Why don't you all come in? Delaney put out some appetizers."

Once we got to the kitchen, he asked, "Can I get anyone a drink? We have beer, wine, pop, water..."

Everyone put in their requests, and while I got wine for my friends, Preston grabbed beer for the guys.

"How did you and Preston decide on a name?" Rayne asked.

I set Paxton on the counter and gave him a plate with chips on it. "Preston came up with it. My mom's name is Evelyn, and my middle name is Marie."

Preston took a drink of his beer. "Her mom started crying when we told her."

"How did his mom take it?" Vivian asked in a low voice.

After Preston and I had told my parents about the two of us getting back together, I'd met with Vivian and Rayne and given them our whole backstory from our divorce to our reunion. I'd also told them about my mother-in-law and how Preston had stood up to her for me.

"She didn't say a word," I said. Which was true, but she'd looked like she'd just finished sucking on a lemon, her mouth pursed so tightly.

Preston snorted. "She was pissed as hell, but a lady never complains." He said the last half with sarcasm.

"Moms, man," Dominick said.

"How is your mom, Dominick?" I asked. "Is your brother still living with you?"

Vivian and Dominick had moved out of her apartment and bought a house together around the time I was selling mine, and since most of my furniture was no longer needed, I sold it to them. With Spencer in high school, they wanted him to have some of his own space, so they'd made sure to purchase a home with a finished basement so he could hang out down there while they had the upstairs more to themselves.

Dominick nodded. "She's doing okay. Once she was well enough to come home, she never even fought me for Spencer to move back in with her. She's been going to AA and NA meetings, but I know she struggles. And Spencer's almost done with his senior year, but Vivian and I told him he could still live with us if he wanted to go to college locally."

"And tell Delaney what else happened recently," Rayne said with a smile.

Vivian rolled her eyes and tried to look annoyed, but I could see the happiness in her eyes when she held up her left hand, showing a simple gold band on her ring finger.

My mouth dropped open. "You got married?"

"Dominick and I took a page out of your book and went to the courthouse."

Dominick grinned. "When I asked her about getting married, she wasn't very excited about it. But once I asked more questions, I realized she didn't care for the idea of a wedding, but she would be fine with marriage. I told her once that she was never getting rid of me, and now, she can't."

"He's like a fungus," Vivian joked.

"You are such a liar," Rayne said. "You're head over heels for him."

Vivian scowled. "*Shh.*"

Not the least bit intimidated by our friend, Rayne laughed.

"Well, I am happy for you both," I said to Vivian and Dominick.

"Same," Preston said. "Congratulations."

"And speaking of weddings, how is the planning going?" I asked Rayne.

She and Cade were getting married in three months.

She nuzzled Everly's dark head. "Everything is mostly planned. It's more of just a countdown now. Cade's almost busier with the restaurant opening next month than with wedding stuff."

"Delaney already asked her family to babysit so we can go out that night," Preston said.

I laughed. "Listen, I've already been home for over six weeks. While I love spending time with my children, I miss being around adults. I'll still be on maternity leave, and I'll be pumping by then, so I'm drinking." I looked sadly at my water. Not that I drank very much when I wasn't pregnant or breastfeeding, but I was the only adult without alcohol in my hands.

Preston tilted his head. "What about me? You seemed to think I was good company last night."

My face heated. Last week, I had gone to my six-week checkup and gotten the all clear for sex. Preston hadn't been able to keep his hands off me since. I knew he'd gone weeks without sex, but I was also convinced he'd also wanted to make sure things were different this time between us. I couldn't love him more for how much he wanted me to know he still cared.

I ignored his sexual innuendo since we were in the company of others. "Yeah, well, you're just one person. And you go to the office a couple times a week, so you get out more than me."

Vivian frowned. "Why don't you do more stuff?" She eyed Preston like he was holding me prisoner or something, but since he was her boss, she managed to keep her mouth shut.

Putting my hand on my husband's arm, I explained, "Preston encourages me to do stuff, and it's not like I don't go anywhere. It's just that the baby nurses so often that it's easier to be close to home. And we don't quite want to start her on bottles yet. But by the restaurant opening, she will be."

"Mommy, can I watch TV?" Paxton asked.

"Go for it." I grabbed his empty plate while he jumped down from the counter and ran into the living room.

"He's adorable," Rayne said. "You really have a beautiful family, Delaney."

Preston turned and pulled me into his arms. I leaned back against his chest, and he kissed the top of my head.

"Thank you, Rayne." I looked up at my handsome husband and smiled. "I like to think so."

I was a very lucky woman. Shifting my gaze to my friends, I watched them with their partners, and it was obvious I wasn't the only lucky one.

TURN THE PAGE FOR A SAMPLE OF

THE D APPOINTMENT

THE D APPOINTMENT
VIVIAN

I hesitated at the end of the walkway up to the small house Gina had given me the address to.

The home was in good shape, but the landscaping left something to be desired. Not that I was there to learn gardening tips. I was there for sex.

I took a deep breath and took my first step forward.

I didn't think of myself as a prude. I didn't really care what people did in their bedrooms as long as it was consensual, but I definitely wasn't adventurous in that area, and I was feeling out of my depth.

Which meant, I had to fake it.

I squared my shoulders before knocking on the door. This Dom guy didn't need to know that I was in unfamiliar territory.

The front door swung open, and a tall blond man stood on the other side. He had a buzzed head and tattoos on his arms. I supposed some women would think he was attractive with his blue eyes and chiseled jaw. But I wasn't one of them. When I'd told Gina I liked clean-cut men, I should have suspected she would ignore me.

I should have never asked her to do me this favor.

But I was stuck, and even though I wanted to turn around and leave, that would be rude. Instead, I pulled up my professional facade I used at work and smiled politely. "Hello. I'm Vivian. Are you Dom?"

The guy eyed me up and down and leaned his head back, shouting, "Dom, some chick is here for you. Her name is..." He looked back at me and raised his brow.

"Vivian."

"Vivian," he finished as he opened the door for me to step inside, and I sighed with relief that this wasn't the guy I was there to hook up with.

"I'll be there in a sec," a deep voice called from the back.

"I'm headed out. Talk to you later," the blond guy yelled again.

"Later, Tony."

The man stepped around me and left without ever introducing himself or saying good-bye to me.

Left alone, I scanned the room and tried not to cringe. I could tell the owner was a bachelor and didn't have a lot of money. The furniture was old and mismatched, but that wasn't what bothered me. It was very messy. There were clothes thrown on the back of the couch, a pile of shoes lay in a heap by the door, a couple of crumb-filled plates sat on the coffee table along with empty beer bottles.

It wasn't exactly dirty, but it was unkempt, and again, I wondered what I was doing there.

The sound of footsteps turned my attention from the living room to the hallway, where a person who had to be Dom stepped out.

I held my breath as the dark-haired man grabbed the ends of the white towel wrapped around his neck and stared at me. A glint in his hazel eyes was followed by him licking his bottom lip, which was full and dark pink. The sexiness flowed off of him like it was a tangible thing I could touch, and I was entranced by him. I was also wet.

"You must be Vivian," he muttered.

Hearing him speak was enough to break me out of my stupor, and I swiftly became aware of the rest of him.

Besides the towel, he only had on a pair of well-worn jeans and a silver chain around his neck with a gold medallion. He had a dark beard that framed his perfect mouth, a nose piercing, an earring, and tattoos that covered not just his arms, but also his chest and his neck.

He was the exact opposite of who I would date in real life—from his home to his appearance. Gina had really missed the mark.

I held up a finger. "One moment, please." Reaching into my purse, I found my phone and pulled it out.

> Me: Gina, is this some kind of joke? I'm sure your friend is perfectly nice, but he isn't my type.

Rather than text me back, Gina called me.

"This is Vivian," I answered.

A deep sigh sounded on the other side. "You are a really hard person to do a favor for."

I winced, feeling guilty. "I apologize. It's just that—"

"Look, do you want to get off, or do you want to find a new boyfriend?"

The question was similar to the one she'd asked me earlier today.

My eyes darted to Dom, and I turned my back to him, as if that would make my conversation more private, before I answered, "The former."

"That's what I thought."

"But—"

"But nothing. Dom is going to give you the best orgasm of your life, and God knows that's exactly what you need."

"Excuse me?"

"And I know you think you're better than him, but, honey, Dom doesn't need you. He can get pussy whenever he wants. There is nothing special about yours, so if I were you, I wouldn't waste this opportunity."

My jaw dropped. I was speechless.

"Should I tell him you've changed your mind, or are you staying?"

My phone was plucked from my hand from behind me, and I spun around, coming face-to-face with Dom's chest. A fleeting thought of what he would taste like if I licked him flashed in my head.

"She's staying," he said into my phone. He hit End,

slipped my bag from my arm, put my cell inside, and set it on the floor.

"How do you know I'm staying?" I asked.

He moved forward, causing me to step back until my butt hit the wall. I swallowed hard.

Dom caged me in with his arms on either side of my head and met my eyes. "Gina said that you need to get laid. That's why you're here, are you not?"

Heat rose to my cheeks. "Yes," I admitted, but I didn't want him to forget the most important part. "But I need a little more than to just get laid."

He tilted his head to the side, not picking up on my subtle hint.

I cleared my throat. "I need to come."

He grinned. "Oh, you'll come all right." He stepped back and bit his lip as he studied me. Grabbing my hand, he pulled me toward the hall. "Let's go."

ABOUT THE AUTHOR

R.L. Kenderson is two best friends writing under one name.

Renae has always loved reading, and in third grade, she wrote her first poem where she learned she might have a knack for this writing thing. Lara remembers sneaking her grandmother's Harlequin novels when she was probably too young to be reading them, and since then, she knew she wanted to write her own.

When they met in college, they bonded over their love of reading and the TV show *Charmed*. What really spiced up their friendship was when Lara introduced Renae to romance novels. When they discovered their first vampire romance, they knew there would always be a special place in their hearts for paranormal romance. After being unable to find certain storylines and characteristics they wanted to read about in the hundreds of books they consumed, they decided to write their own.

One lives in the Minneapolis-St. Paul area and the other in the Kansas City area where they both work in the medical field during the day and a sexy author by night. They communicate through phone, email, and whole lot of messaging.

You can find them at http://www.rlkenderson.com, Facebook, Instagram, TikTok, and Goodreads. Join their reader group! Or you can email them at rlkenderson@ rlkenderson.com, or sign up for their newsletter. They always love hearing from their readers.

Manufactured by Amazon.ca
Acheson, AB